ERASMUS PLUMWOOD

Other Books by the same Author

THE ADVENTURES OF HORATIO WOOSENCRAFT AND OTHER
SHORT STORIES

TRAVELS IN TIME ACROSS EUROPE

Erasmus Plumwood.

a novel

by

Seán Thomas Kane

Published by the Author

Kansas City, Missouri, United States

ISBN: 978-0578404189

For all of my friends
who take great delight
in the following chapters
long into the night.

Pour tous de mes amis
qui aiment beaucoup ces chapitres
et lisent leurs tout le nuit
cet œuvre est mon cadeau pour vous.

CONTENTS

Introduction

I've wanted to write a novel since I began writing poetry my freshman year of high school at Saint James Academy. At that point I was fascinated with Robert Burns, and began to develop my own style based upon his Scots mannerisms. I loved reading his poem "Tam o' Shanter", which admittedly influenced some of my choices for the two main characters in this book. As the years have progressed, I have steadily begun to build up more stamina as a writer, and have been able to extend the depth of my ink further on the page, allowing for more detailed writing, that has extended my stories and chapters from a mere half-page to the thirty and forty page behemoths that made up some of the longer parts of my last book *Travels in Time Across Europe*. While writing that book, I had some ideas for a novel that would appear here or there and took note of most of them. There are a few ideas that started at that point in 2016 that have made their way into this volume, yet for the most part the events detailed in *Erasmus Plumwood* are largely based upon real events from my own life and a vacation that I took with my parents and a family friend up to the Christmas Farm and Inn in Jackson, New Hampshire between 17 and 21 December 2017.

As we were leaving Kansas City very early on the morning of Sunday, 17 December, I was in a bad mood. I had planned on spending my birthday, the twentieth, at my favourite cinema in Downtown Kansas City watching the latest *Star Wars* film with my family and friends, as I had spent my birthdays in 2015 and 2016. I wanted to make a tradition out of it and looked forward to enjoying the simple pleasures of being at home on that most important day in my year. Yet my Mom and our family friend decided it would be fun to travel up to this Christmas Inn in the White Mountains of New Hampshire that week.

I agreed to it, and went along, despite not entirely wanting to travel halfway across the continent to spend my birthday in the snow. And while I spent most of the week sick with a cold, I nevertheless discovered a corner of the country that I had never seen before; it is a region that has left an indelible mark on my mind, and one where I would happily abscond to for good, if I could find a job up there near Conway or Jackson as a historian or professor.

This book has far too many influences to name in one short page, but I hope you enjoy reading it. I hope you enjoy this book as much as I have enjoyed writing it.

—— Seán Thomas Kane
Kansas City, September 2018.

1

On the Upper West Side

"The train approaching is the 1 train to South Ferry, please stand back."

Erasmus heeded the customary station announcement warning only just, doing as most of the regular commuters on the platform did and standing by, waiting to jump at the opportunity to board on their commute home. It had been another day at Columbia, another day near the end of his Master's with defences and meetings. His students were lining up at the door to the TA Office trying to get some help for their final exam, one that nearly everyone was dreading. This was the most basic course that the Computer Science class could have offered, an Introduction to Coding, yet many of the students who signed up for it still four months after the semester's commencement in September were at a loss when they had to write code.

At the end of the day Erasmus had sat back in his swivel chair; the windowless office felt ready to be abandoned for the evening. It was Wednesday, a cold Wednesday evening not far from the breezy Hudson. Though deep inside the bowels of the Computer Science Building, Erasmus' ears could easily imagine the traffic on the great avenues and streets outside as Manhattan's grid quickly began to swell with the evening rush hour fast approaching. Looking at his computer screen once more, his email opened up for the continued trickle of worried students to reach him rapidly, Erasmus sighed, "Alright, I think that's enough for today." He closed down the browser that his email had been opened in and signed out of his computer with a quick succession of keystrokes that his hands had known almost as well as the texture of his fingertips: control alt delete. Those three keys were the signal to his brain: time to leave.

Erasmus stood from his chair, and with a step backwards he replaced his light blue suit coat onto his shoulders, that gentle soft-purple woollen scarf over his neck like a priest's shawl, and his finely framed dark green overcoat thus over the scarf. Fully dressed and covered from the impending cold, Erasmus took his black leather briefcase in hand and walked out of his office, letting the door close behind him, the lock activating once the door had shut. He turned right and strode down the now dimly lit hall, about the corner and to the right again down the main hall that served as spine to the lowest level of the basement of the Computer Science Building. At the middle of the hall Erasmus looked at the stairs, but with a sense of exhaustion that is native to the end of the day he turned about and pressed the up button to call for the elevator instead.

The old car slowly earked its way down, the cables seeming

to grind as they undertook that same motion they had done for three generations of computer scientists and engineers that had undertaken their studies and research at Columbia. After three minutes, Erasmus began to have his daily thought that maybe it would have just been quicker to take the stairs; the elevator reached the basement and opened its mouth, an odour of postwar memories emanating from within the wooden and metal car. Erasmus stepped through the open jaws and turned to the left, pressing the (1) button to ascend to street level once more. The old custodian of the building's acrophobes and handicapped daytime occupants let an audible sigh at the summons echoing from the first-floor button that was placed just within its corpus. Mustering up its energies the mouth closed with a klang and gave itself a moment to catch its breath before ascending the cables with the desire for rest that one would expect of a weary veteran of service in the lifting industry.

Erasmus waited patiently, knowing this elevator's limitations, he leaned on the rail in the back of the elevator, figuring the process of ascending one floor would take a little longer. As the elevator pulled its way closer to the stars up the cables Erasmus prepared himself for what was next, a brisk walk a few blocks to the subway. The weather broadcast that morning on the radio called for temperatures well below freezing, yet for the millions of New Yorkers who would take to the streets that day this lowering of the temperature would be nothing out of the ordinary for a brisk mid-December day.

The elevator once more loosened its jaws and allowed Erasmus to eject himself from its body into the main lobby of the building. The Kansas Citian turned his back on the front doors of the building and made his way southwards along a corridor lined with classrooms and offices towards a back entrance to the building. There he exited out the large glass doors and made his way briskly across the adjacent courtyard and down a pedestrian footpath alongside the business and sciences buildings. At the trees he took a right and strode briskly, with purpose, along the broad-walk at the heart of the campus, past the Mathematics Department and along the backside of the great dome so often portrayed on postcards and in film. At Broadway he turned left, heading south towards the Subway entrance at 116th Street. The grey masonry at street level contrasted with the nineteenth-century red brick of the upper levels of these same buildings, their edifices announcing the elite nature of this colonial institution. Just before 116th Street he made a sharp turn and descended downwards into the subway, the green railings matching the old lamppost that kept that station awash and illuminated at night.

Once inside Erasmus made his way, now memorised after countless days and nights of making the same path, through the turnstiles and down onto the southbound platform. He stood and waited, less patiently more resignedly at the fact of his current situation. Not more than two minutes passed before a train came roaring into the station on the local tracks, slowing to a stop at the platform before him. The doors slid open with their customary bang, and Erasmus stood back as those commuters arriving for their night classes and quiet evenings in their apartments disembarked before himself boarding the train and taking his place near a handrail alongside countless others, all in their own worlds, their brief, unspoken, unadmitted companionship a regular if unrecognised part of their day. The train doors slid shut, prompting all to subconsciously ready themselves to begin to move once more ever further south towards downtown.

As the 1 Train barrelled along towards Cathedral Parkway, Erasmus drew his phone from his pocket and began checking his email. He hadn't looked at his private account in a while, only keeping tabs on his university address during that busy day at the office. Unsurprisingly, 42 emails awaited his observation, 37 of which were readily trashable, leaving a mere five that bore any interest to the soon-graduate. As the doors slid open at 103rd Street Erasmus opened one email from an address that he did not recognise, but that nevertheless looked interesting enough to pass the remaining four minutes that he had in the company of these fine, if muted, commuters.

"Dear Mr. Plumwood,

Thank you for your application for the position of Business Development Manager. We have considered your application and would like to invite you to join us for an interview tomorrow (14 December) by phone. We will be available to interview you anytime between 3:00 and 4:00 pm Pacific time. Please respond if you are still interested in this post by choosing an interview time via our online scheduling programme. If you have any questions, please don't hesitate to call me at 415-555-3267.

Regards,
Bruce Tybald
H.R. Manager

Technophilia Inc.
450 Pine Street, Ste. 2307
San Francisco, CA 94108"

Erasmus didn't know what to say, he expected that he'd get some interviews, but never at such a lauded company as Technophilia. He'd expected to stay in New York, or maybe go back to Kansas City. Still, Erasmus had applied for jobs throughout the U. S. and back in England as well. He would take advantage of his dual citizenship as long as it was allowed. *"Technophilia,"* he thought, *"I might be moving to San Francisco!"*

"This is 79th Street."

Erasmus had been taken aback by how quickly the train had made its way down from Columbia. He pushed his way without much protest out of the subway car and onto his home platform, walking at a slightly less brisk pace towards the exit to street-level. Ascending back up onto Broadway, he crossed the great thoroughfare and made his way eastwards on 79th Street, crossing Amsterdam Avenue and turning right there to head southwards again, taking another left onto 76th Street to his apartment just past the synagogue. Fumbling as he did everyday with his keys, Erasmus found the right one and let himself into the big front door of his building, this time climbing the stairs up three floors to his apartment that faced out towards the alley behind the building.

Unlocking the door Erasmus could smell what seemed like a nice mushroom sauce heating up on the stove. He walked in, closed the door, hung up his coat and scarf on his hook, and strode into the kitchen to the sight of his roommate and best friend Marie-Thérèse at work. She wore her moderately-lengthed brunette hair back in a ponytail so as to keep it from interrupting with her work. Her mild yellow long sweater and black leggings were covered by a plain brown apron, which hung from about her neck down to just at her knees. She wore a simple, functional pair of flats on her feet, their blue and white pattern reminiscent of the flag of her native province of Québec. As Erasmus entered the kitchen, Marie-Thérèse turned to greet him with a casual, everyday smile.

"Hey there, you're home early!" he said in surprise.

"Well, when my students don't come to ask me questions, then I can presume they don't need my help," she said in her sweet *Montréalaise* accent.

"Wish I could say the same."

"Your subject is just more abstract than my own."

"I suppose you're right," he said considering the differences between teaching French and teaching computer coding. "But they're both languages, *mais non ?* »

« *Oui, mon ami*, but my language developed naturally, yours was only invented in the last few decades."

"All the more reason to learn it."

"It'll help them find jobs."

"Indeed it will," thought Erasmus, still mulling that email he had received from Technophilia. "What're you making?"

"A favourite that I had in France, *escalope du poulet avec un sauce forestiers*. »

"It smells delightful," Erasmus cried with a big cheesy smile.

Marie-Thérèse examined his face, "You look occupied, are your students unprepared for the exam?"

Erasmus looked at the sink, "No, it's not that. I heard back from Technophilia today. They want to interview me tomorrow."

"Tomorrow! *Excellent* Erasmus, that's great news!" Marie-Thérèse shouted, nearly jumping from her pan of mushroom sauce on the stove to give her friend a hug.

Erasmus smiled, the warm embrace of the friend closest to his heart made the whole day feel all the more better."

"I take it your interview will be over the phone? You surely can't fly out to San Francisco in time for it," Marie-Thérèse said with a wry smile.

"Yes, I need to go and schedule that now actually. They have an online system for doing this sort of scheduling."

Erasmus pulled out his phone, pulling up the email again and clicking on the link to take him to the scheduling page.

"When do they want to talk with you?"

"Between 3:00 and 4:00 Pacific time tomorrow, so between 6:00 and 7:00 our time."

"Well, that won't interfere with your classes," she said turning some of the sauce about with a wooden spoon.

"No, but it'll be later in the evening than I would've liked."

"Ah don't worry, Erasmus, just keep it to one glass of wine tomorrow and you'll be fine," Marie-Thérèse said with a laugh.

"Only one, why that - that's entirely unfair!" Erasmus cried in his best petulant old man impression.

"Entirely unfair, em... *oui*, but you have an interview to give and they'll expect to be speaking to a man who isn't too terribly tipsy."

« *D'accord, mon amie* » he sighed, admitting defeat, though with the hint of a grin on his face. "That sauce really does smell divine!"

"You're right, it does. But you smell like the 1 Train. Why don't you go wash your hands off and I'll get this dinner ready for us," Marie-Thérèse said, pointing her sauced spoon at the Missourian.

Erasmus took a deep, Louis XIV era bow, "Milady," he sighed before lowering his hands to his sides and turning about to the bathroom around the corner. He washed his hands and listened as the sauce sizzled in the pan, dancing with the oil like two ballerinas partaking in a sea lion choral contest.

Returning from the lavatory, Erasmus set himself into the kitchen to acquire a pair of plates, some cutlery, and a pair of wine glasses for their evening's meal that seemed to be mushrooming into quite the affair. Not only did Marie-Thérèse have a forestiers sauce bubbling in the pan like a drunken Methodist, she also was preparing what looked to be a bread pudding in the oven for dessert.

Marie-Thérèse took one last twirl of the sauce and pressed a spatula down on the chicken cooking in an adjacent pan, confirming its readiness for consumption. With a motion smoother than milk pouring from a bottle she glided the four pieces of chicken in pairs onto the pair of plates that Erasmus had placed on the countertop beside the stove. She then gently poured the forestiers sauce over the chicken with her wooden spoon in a manner befitting an expert of the art of fondue. The main course in place, Marie-Thérèse went to a nearby pot that had been steaming broccoli, carrots, beans, and asparagus and offered a liberal amount to each plate. She handed the plates off to Erasmus, who faithfully attended his friend with the food. Turning about carefully, Erasmus set the plates on opposite sides of the round table that marked the separation between the kitchen and living room of their apartment.

Erasmus waited for Marie-Thérèse to pass from the kitchen to the table before pulling back his chair and sitting, having learned his manners from the best in his own family. His Aunt Delia, a fine woman of good character who had nearly seen the twentieth-century through could teach him all he needed to know of table manners. As he sat Erasmus took hold of the fine Beaujolais that was in perfect season and withdrew the already loose-lipped cork from the bottleneck with an ever-refreshing swepop emanating from the neck. Placing the cork on the table, Erasmus delicately poured the vintage from its glass confines, the vessel within which it had travelled across the Atlantic from the banks of the Saône to their little apartment within smell-o-vision reach of the Hudson, into Marie-Thérèse's glass with a smoothness only discovered after years of getting it wrong and bleeding the blessed fruit over many a tablecloth. The Montréalaise was as pleased as ever with her roommate's pouring abilities and looked on as he fed his own glass with the same Bacchanalian nectar. On an evening of greater celebration or commiseration Erasmus might well have filled his glass nearly to its rim, but with a sweet sense of normality and calm he only half-filled it, to the same degree as Marie-Thérèse's had been so half-fulfilled.

"It looks good," Erasmus said, taking his knife and fork in hand and strategizing his next move.

"Looks aren't everything, try eating it," Marie-Thérèse replied, cutting her chicken with a ravenous rapidity that mirrored her sharp-edged sarcasm.

"Why is this called forestiers sauce?" Erasmus asked, similarly slicing his twin large pieces of chicken into smaller pieces.

"I'm not sure," replied the chef, her own fork now fully loaded with a moderate-sized piece of chicken dripping tenderly with the mushroom sauce like one of Ziegfeld's showgirls dripping with pearls.

"Hm," came the Midwesterner's reply as he inserted a bit of her chicken into his mouth.

Erasmus and Marie-Thérèse chewed away for a whole four measures at a dotted ¾ beat. Soon enough their chewing was in unison, their jaws dancing in a common rhythm and motion, as if in they waltzed together in Stephansplatz in the heart of Vienna. Then as if acting out a dinner dance both set down their forks *au même temps* and replaced them in hand with their glasses, taking a nice, deep drink of wine before returning the glasses to their places at the top right corner of their plates, restoring the forks to their rightful duties among their pale fingers, now back to their hard labour assaulting the pieces of chicken before them.

With each bite the twin plates became barer and barer, nearly naked if not for the remnants of sauce that adorned their white porcelain faces. Soon though the diners caught onto the amusing harmony with which their eating habits mirrored each other. Marie-Thérèse broke into a fine maritime hornpipe, her teeth chomping down with feminine elegance to the same beat as the famed *Sailor's Hornpipe*, while Erasmus supplied a good secondary beat, both taking long drinks of their wine at the end of the second parts of each verse. What perhaps would have surprised the third-party observer most was that neither of the two broke a smile or forced wine from their mouths into their noses out of laughter, as is sometimes known to happen, but rather continued on their merry dental dinner dance regardless of the tandem humour ensuing within their mouths.

As their dinner reached the summit of its intensity, the customary small talk recommenced. Marie-Thérèse held her glass of wine tenderly in her fingers, the rounded petal of the glass hardly brushing her palm. Erasmus sat back in his chair, breathing curtly, considering his options with Technophilia.

"You're nervous, aren't you?"

"I just don't know if this is best for me," Erasmus replied, letting his hands fall onto his thighs, his eyes darting upwards to look at her face.

"It's an excellent first job in your field, a great way to start your career."

"I just don't know if I'm ready to leave New York," he replied with a soulful glance out the window behind Marie-Thérèse.

Marie-Thérèse put down her glass and thought about this island city. "It really is such an amazing place. Neither of us are from a city quite like it. I mean, Montréal is bigger than Kansas City, but it's hardly on the same scale as New York."

"There's so much life here," his eyes darting downwards from the window to meet hers, "so much opportunity. Everyday there's something new to be excited about."

"You always knew that you couldn't stay at Columbia forever."

"But Columbia is only a small part of this city. I could find a company to take me on here, I mean, I already live in Manhattan, I wouldn't have to move from somewhere out west just to come work in New York!" Erasmus' voice was raised, in a sense abrasive.

"San Francisco's not so bad though," Marie-Thérèse replied softly, noting the trepidation in her best friend's voice. "Sure it's not as big as New York, and the weather's completely different, but it's still a big city full of life and people and new ideas –"

"But you won't be living there—"

Erasmus thought what he didn't want to say. He looked at Marie-Thérèse as his best and dearest friend, the one who understood him, who got him. Yet all the same Erasmus didn't want to seem desperate to be with her, he didn't want their friendship to move in anyway down that road. After all, it didn't seem like Marie-Thérèse was in the mood for a change in their hitherto platonic relationship. She was the same old Marie-Thérèse, always on the move, always solving puzzles like Erasmus' hero Alan Turing.

As he pondered, Erasmus had lost focus on his surroundings. Marie-Thérèse was saying something, though he hadn't heard a word. Yet as he refocused his vision Erasmus couldn't help but notice her eyes, their piercing brown looking directly back at him with a sharp gentleness that meant Marie-Thérèse had asked him a question. "I'm sorry, what'd you say?" Erasmus asked, looking mellowly into those orbs of brown.

"I was just saying that I think we need a vacation," came the reply.

"A vacation?"

"Yes. Listen to yourself; you're worrying yourself sick about this job offer. You need to take a break for a few days and relax. And trust me, just because I got off work early today doesn't mean I'm stress free. Let's go away next week, to somewhere we haven't been yet."

"Where're you thinking? Rajasthan?" came the Kansas Citian's sarcasm.

"To India for less than a week? Are you crazy?" flew the retort.

"Yes. Next question."

"How about we go up into the mountains, in New Hampshire. My friend Jeanne-Louise told me about this inn up in the Mt. Washington Valley that's Christmas themed. They even have a spa. We could go up there for a few nights and just get away from things."

"Do we have the budget for this?" Erasmus replied, considerate of the offer but nevertheless a constant conservationist with the contents of his pocketbook.

"Don't worry about that. Consider this your Christmas present," Marie-Thérèse replied, taking her phone from the table and looking up the Inn in question.

"Well, I guess I should look for a new present of equal worth then," Erasmus sighed wryly.

"Why, what'd you get me?" Marie-Thérèse asked.

"A bunny."

"Really?!" Marie-Thérèse cried with a sense of joy.

"No."

« *Merde.* You really can be an ass sometimes, Erasmus Plumwood," she replied with an only half-fake pout.

"I know," he responded, rising from the table to collect their plates and return them to the kitchen for cleaning.

Marie-Thérèse returned to her phone as Erasmus opened the faucet with a pull of the handle, letting cool New York tap water rush down the spout and onto the plates and cutlery. He washed the lot and placed each item in its turn in the drying rack on the countertop. Closing the dishwasher tightly and letting it commence its cycle, Erasmus walked back towards Marie-Thérèse, this time passing the table and taking a well-reclined seat on the sofa beyond, in front of the TV, whose black screen remained so unenlightened by Erasmus' desire for amusement.

"So this place is called the Noel Inn," Marie-Thérèse said, peering down at her phone screen. "It's in a village called Jackson, New Hampshire. Looks like it's pretty close to Mt. Washington."

"How far is it from here?" Erasmus asked, turning around slightly on the black leather sofa to look at Marie-Thérèse.

"Not too far. Why don't you figure out how we're going to get there," she replied, setting down her phone on the table and standing. She removed her apron and let it hang over the backrest of her chair, pushing the chair in so it didn't stick out in their smallish apartment. Having reset the chair she walked over to the sofa, plopping down in it with a sense of sleepiness yet relief at the end of yet another week.

Erasmus pulled out his own phone from his pocket to figure out how to get to Jackson, New Hampshire. Surely it wasn't too difficult to get to. He quickly found driving directions, but wasn't in much of a mood for a long journey. Seeing that a flight made little sense he decided to check the railways. Sure enough, there was an easy way to get close to Jackson by train.

"I think I've got it," he said, holding his phone aloft in his hand, turning his head to look at Marie-Thérèse, who had laid her own head down on the soft back of the sofa, her eyes half closed.

"How're we going to get there?" she asked.

"By train, with one connection in Portland."

She raised her head and gave him a quizzical look, "Portland, Oregon?"

"No, the other one. Portland, Maine."

"O, ok. Sounds good to me," she laid her head back down, "Book the tickets then. I'll take care of the Inn in a few moments."

Before she could finish the momentous last word her voice began to drift off into a sweet slumber, one she had been looking forward to for quite sometime.

Erasmus sat there, looking at the empty fireplace before him. He realised that in the six years they had lived together in that apartment they had yet to actually use their fireplace for its intended incandescent purpose. Looking more closely at it, Erasmus decided it might be a good idea, on such a cold December evening, to have a fire. "Just make sure it stays in the fireplace and doesn't bring down the rest of the building," he muttered, standing and walking over towards the thick concrete cavern in the eastern wall of their abode.

Kneeling down, he peered into its aperture and discerned the place where he could place some wood or kindling to ignite his desires. Yet where to get the wood? Central Park? No, that's a felony-worthy offence. Maybe there's a shop around that sells firewood? Erasmus put his hand to his trouser pocket to extract his phone only to find it away from home. He looked up and saw it resting where he had left it on the arm of the sofa next to his previous seat.

Sighing, Erasmus pushed himself heavenward with his hands firmly pressed against the ground, pushing up. Restoring his figure upon its feet, he heard his knees give a loud, relieving pop as they straightened from their hitherto bent figure. Stepping forward gingerly, still a bit dizzy in the head from his sudden ascent from a seated position at around 70 cm up to his regular height of 173 cm, Erasmus took the three steps back across the room to the sofa, retrieved his phone and unlocked it, opening a browser window thereupon. With a quick, natural pace, he typed into the search browser "Firewood UWS NYC," getting only three results, each of which were on the far side of Manhattan near the East River. "I don't want to go out," he muttered with a grimace, locking his phone again and resuming his prior seat on the sofa, staring at that empty fireplace before him.

Marie-Thérèse muttered something in French about « cochons » in her sleep. Erasmus looked over at her again, the semi-autonomous strands of her soft brunette falling gently over her neck, their hue fading into her pale skin. She seemed eager to go up to New Hampshire, to this mountain inn place. Erasmus took the laptop that had sat atop their coffee table since its last use the night prior and opened it, restoring it to life and vibrancy. With a mechanical flash of light and colour it came on, and greeted the master coder with the usual lock screen. Choosing his profile and unlocking his account, Erasmus came to his homepage, its background a fond reminder of youthful wonders at home, the Great Buddha at the Nelson-Atkins Museum in Kansas City, a favourite of generations in his family going back to before the Second World War.

Moving past the home screen as always, Erasmus opened a web browser and searched for the Noel Inn in Jackson, New Hampshire. "That's a nice name," he mused as he found himself inside the inn's website. Looking to see what sort of rooms were on offer, Erasmus quickly discovered he would have no shortage of twin double bed rooms available. Yet each room appeared to have its own unique décor and furnishings. Quickly choosing a room that looked nice enough to him, Erasmus entered his card information into the online payment system and looked over at Marie-Thérèse, who was just stirring from her slumber.

« Bonsoir, mon amie, » Erasmus gently hearkened.

« Qu'est que c'est le temps ? » came the Montréalaise's groggy reply.

"It's nearing eight," she sighed placidly, opening her eyes. "I'm booking the room at the Noel Inn for us."

Marie-Thérèse sat up, looking at the bright computer screen. "How much is the room?"

"$99 a night."

"Not bad, not bad," she said, with a hint of impatience at Erasmus' finger's continued hovering over the mousepad, the digital rodent hovering over the equally digital "Book" button on the screen. "Book it, E.!" she exclaimed with a grin reminiscent of her favourite cop show.

Erasmus pressed the book button and watched as the transaction was processed online, until after a half-minute the "Booking Confirmed" screen appeared before the four eyes.

"Alright," Erasmus breathed, "now we just need to find a way up there."

Marie-Thérèse thought for a moment about this rather important technicality. "Let's not fly, the airports are insane this time of year."

"Agreed," nodded the Missourian. "Do you want to rent a car?"

"Maybe once we're up there," she audibly thought, "I don't really want to have to drive the whole way up. I've driven my parents down here from Montréal before. It wasn't fun."

"Yeah, I was never terribly fond of driving from Kansas City to Chicago as a kid," Erasmus concurred.

"How about the railways? What's the closest station to Jackson?"

"Let me look," Erasmus replied, opening a new tab and going to the national railway's website. He searched for New Hampshire and soon found one proximate to the village in question. "How about this one, North Conway, it's a short drive from Jackson. Looks like a nice town for shopping and sightseeing."

"How far of a drive is it?" Marie-Thérèse inquired sceptically.

"O it's only about fifteen minutes," Erasmus reassured his friend.

"That's not bad. It'll take us longer to get to Penn Station from here."

"Quite possibly."

"Alright, let's book the train tickets then," Marie-Thérèse decreed, looking at the screen as Erasmus began to fill in the necessary boxes.

Trip: Round-Trip.
From: New York, NY – Penn Station.
To: North Conway, NH.
Depart: 17 December 2017.
Return: 21 December 2017.
Traveller: 2.

The screen changed, offering the pair two different trains on their chosen travel date. Erasmus and Marie-Thérèse looked closely at what was on offer. The first one left New York at 08:15 in the morning and arrived in North Conway, with one half-hour connection in Portland, Maine at 16:34 in the afternoon. Marie-Thérèse looked at Erasmus, "Well it's a full day of travel but it'll be fun, and far more relaxing than driving!"

"Fair enough, though the price tag is a bit daunting," Erasmus moaned, the $300 tag for two standard class passengers seeming a bit much for the frugal coder.

"Consider this a Christmas treat," Marie-Thérèse reassured him excitedly, her mind already flashing images of the two of them sitting together on a train flying past the fields and forests of New England on their way up to the White Mountains."

"A Christmas treat, well, I guess it's Christmas time isn't it, things are bound to be a bit more expensive now than usual," he capitulated, "Alright then, let's take the train," perking up a smile to his exuberant Québécois friend, "Like you said, it'll be fun!"

"We should probably rent a car once we're in North Conway though," Marie-Thérèse contended. "I doubt they have much public transit up there."

"Probably a good idea," Erasmus agreed, booking the train tickets and changing gears to look for a car rental facility in North Conway. After only a few short keystrokes he made his announcement, as proud as Carter in the Valley of the Kings, "Lucky for us there's one in the town."

"Only one?"

"Only one."

"Must be a small place," Marie-Thérèse exhaled, leaning forward to see better where their rental car would come from.

"Do you want an SUV, seeing as we'll be up in the mountains, or something smaller?"

"The SUV will do, I suppose, could be necessary in the snow up there."

"Right so," Erasmus chose their vehicle, and with another $200 withdrawn, closed his computer and took in a breath. "It's done."

"We're going to the White Mountains," Marie-Thérèse cried, excitement uncontrollable in her voice. She noticed the resignation in his face, resignation at the large block of money just removed from his account. "Don't worry, Erasmus, I'll pay you back. I'll cover the train."

"Sounds good to me," he replied, a sense of relief rushing over his face.

Extracting her phone from its home Marie-Thérèse quickly transferred the $300 to Erasmus' account from her own, and took to her feet. "I don't know about you, but I think this has been a successful evening."

"Yeah, it has, and it's only eight 'o clock," Erasmus confirmed. "What should we do now?"

"Rabbit show jumping?"

"Rabbit what?" Erasmus asked, raising an eyebrow with the grace of a bemused bison meeting a horse for the first time out on the open prairie.

"Rabbit show jumping," Marie-Thérèse confirmed grinning.

"I thought rabbits were born knowing how to jump."

"They learn from their parents."

"Are there many foundling rabbits on the Upper West Side?"

"No, they mostly stick to Washington Square Park."

Erasmus attempted to wrap his mind around the image of hordes of orphaned rabbits hopping about under the arch in Washington Square Park, some with the cunning showiness of a long-eared Beowulf exalting his beot across Heorot to the demonic monster Grendel in the doorway. Unlike the hero of the Geats, the coder of the Missourians was less able. "Why would rabbits want to learn to jump from humans?"

"You should leave your *laboratoire* more often, Erasmus."

"Yeah, the night janitor tells me that about once a week."

« *Le gardien de la nuit ? Vraiment,* Erasmus, you need to give yourself more time to rest!"

"Rest is for engineers," Erasmus replied with a wryly designed grin.

"How many hours did you sleep last night?"

"Five, if you must know, mother."

Marie-Thérèse shot a piercing look at her friend at that maternal title, "Well, no matter what you may think of the pillow and those pesky things called dreams, you need more of them."

"To be honest, I don't know when I'm dreaming, after all what is the difference between a dream and reality?"

« *Comment ?* » the Québécoise asked with an air of apprehension that a freshman philosophy student expresses upon hearing of Sartre's paperknife.

"Well, I often wonder at night if I'm really sleeping or if I'm actually awake but just not physically moving. I mean all day long I work with code, and at night when I'm lying in my bed I find myself thinking in code too."

"You dream in code?" now even the Francophone was questioning the existentiality of her friend's ability to exit from his work.

"I suppose I do. That explains why there have been so many round faces in my dreams, they're all zeroes."

« *Ô zut alors !* We are absolutely going on this vacation to New Hampshire."

Erasmus sighed as Marie-Thérèse stood and began to make her way out of the living room towards the hall that led from the front door to their dining table which sat betwixt the twin pinnacles of their domestic life that were the living room and the kitchen. *"Sure, I spend too much time at work, too much time coding, but what else am I going to do? This is my job, and I need money to live off of, to eat off of, to get that drone so I can freak out the downstairs neighbour's cat,"* he thought as Marie-Thérèse rounded the corner and walked across the hall to the right into her room.

"O, and Erasmus, don't expect your laptop to be in your luggage, 'cause this'll be a technology free week!" she shouted back over her shoulder from her doorway.

The door closed with a finality. Looking at the rental car confirmation page on the screen before him, he muttered with expatriation, « *Ô zut alors* indeed!"

2

"Over Land and River"

Sunday morning came quietly, the bells of the churches a few blocks away ringing in the distance, muffled slightly by the trees and buildings lying in between. As the Mass-goers and church-attendees made their way down the sidewalks of the great city towards their respective churches, Erasmus turned off his back onto his side in bed. *"I'd forgotten how comfy these sheets were, and this blanket as well. Boy, that really feels nice!"* he thought as he turned about.

His room was lit only just by the pale Winter Sun that glowed about the curve of the Earth at a sharp angle expected of morning in New York. The faint sight of Venus was noticed by Melanie Kroneberg, an astrophysicist next door, who often could be found early on winter mornings out on the fire escape just beyond the windows of their building on the south side. Peering through her telescope, Mel smiled with relief at espying the Morning Star in its natural place, orbiting the Sun like our own rocky orb. The faint selenid shadow of the Moon could be seen reflecting to the west across the Hudson over New Jersey, if not as far as the Lehigh Valley across the Delaware in Pennsylvania. Its curved face seemed to still sing its nocturnal hymn, a melody devised by the Divine to warm the hearts of Earth's mortal inhabitants on those cold nights when only the Moon and stars offered warmth from above.

Mel watched through her lens as far above him the warm approach of Phaëton's chariot hearkened with its trumpetous rays the coming of the new day. The bells preceded the coming of the Sun merely thanks to the change in mortal aspiration from allowing nature to dictate the pace of life and time to enforcing rigid structures for the benefit of human comprehension upon the natural mysteries of time. Mel stilled her body and mind for a moment and listened intently to the streets below his perch, from which he could hear the yawning and slowed footsteps of a city awake, but only because their digital and mechanical clocks forced them from the blissful satisfaction of their beds.

"Liberty is independence from the digital watch and smartphone," Mel muttered to herself.

She looked towards Erasmus and Marie-Thérèse's windows next to her own. In the first window Mel saw the Montréalaise hurrying about, packing what she deemed necessary in her suitcase. "Marie-Thérèse Merlinais, always busy with something," she muttered dismissively. She could see no stirring from the second window, whose occupant continued to dream in stirring passages of zeroes and ones.

"Now there's a man who's free. Erasmus Plumwood, and what a man is he! Why, who else could reprogram a parking cop's smartphone so that it —"

RRRRRRRIIIIINNNNNNNNGGGGGG

"— Damn," Mel sighed, leaning back in her chair before turning to the telescope, lining up his left eye with its spyglass, "Never mind. Erasmus Plumwood has an alarm clock. He's just like all the others, a servant to the machine!"

The ringing had not yet subsided but continued in full bruyance. Mel let out an audible sigh that startled a sleepwalker heading to Holy Trinity Episcopalian Church two blocks away. "What have they been feeding the squirrels on this block?" the sleepwalking Episcopalian cried, looking up into the tree that was rooted in front of the building.

Nevertheless, Erasmus's alarm continued to sound. It's ringing awoke all the frustration that Mel felt for the modern world, for its slaves to the machine. She stood from her telescope, walked gingerly barefoot along the cold rails of the fire escape, and knocked hard on Erasmus's window. "Erasmus Plumwood, you ballard! Turn off that alarm!"

Erasmus regained focus for all things that were not his sheets and blankets and listened for a moment. What did Mel want this time?

"Erasmus, shut that up!" Mel shouted from her perch on the fire escape.

Erasmus lay there, unsure what she was talking about. A ringing seemed to have encompassed his ears. It felt slightly less nice than his pillow, though it reminded him of that lamp that continued to buzz with electricity in his basement office up at Columbia.

A loud knock came on the door, then its hinges creaked open with a start. "Erasmus, wake up, we need to go to Penn Station!"

"What are we doing there, M.T.?"

"Going to New Hampshire, don't you remember, our *vacances* ?"

"New Hampshire," Erasmus thought, *"why the hell would I want to go there?"*

He then remembered the rental car and the country inn. "O yeah, New Hampshire," he replied, taking the alarm by its handle and flipping the switch in the back to shut it off.

He laid back on his pillow for one last moment of exaltation. "Alright, then. Give me a few minutes."

Marie-Thérèse backed out from the room, closing the door behind her. Erasmus rose from his bed, stretched his neck and walked to the window, drawing back the curtains and opening the glass he hailed his neighbour, "G'morning, Mel. Did you sleep well?"

"Better than you, I should think," Mel retorted, an air of disgust emanating from her tone and words.

"That's good," Erasmus muttered, turning about from the window and the astrophysicist on the fire escape and walking back towards his wardrobe, which stood to the right of his bed on the far wall of the room from the door. The soft golden-red shade of paint upon the room's walls sparkled in the waxing light of the Sun like Oberon and Tatiana's subjects dancing about in their silvian abode. Having woken up to this same sight for nigh two years now, Erasmus no longer noticed the ethereal luminescent dance taking place amidst the specks of paint upon his walls.

He walked across the hard-wooden floorboards that completed the cubed shape of his room. Their wood was a darker stain that matched the Victorian sensibilities of interior design that were prevalent in the late nineteenth century when his building on 76th Street was first erected. How else had Erasmus and Marie-Thérèse gotten this apartment for so cheap, especially on the Upper West Side? It had hardly been updated since the Eisenhower administration, and there was still the odd bit of paint here or there, especially in the closets, that dated from the days when Teddy Roosevelt was chief executive and primary resident at 1600 Pennsylvania Avenue NW. Erasmus had marvelled in the past at how some of these materials had survived for so long, despite the city around them always on the move. New skyscrapers rose up and down Manhattan, they were always taller, always made of more glass, and now far narrower. Yet despite this, in the back corners, in the closets of forgotten apartments in a quiet residential corner of the city there still remained in constant everyday use some echoes of a now long forgotten time.

Erasmus opened his wardrobe and, without need of his eyes, withdrew a set of underclothes to commence his morning routine. In these next thirty minutes, Erasmus was the least uncommon person along the East Coast of the Americas. His feet mumbled their way out their dreaming-chamber, across the corridor into the lavatory, to the apartment's thinking-seat, upon which he took his place, his mind on other things. That morning, Erasmus thought about drones. *"What makes a drone fly so smoothly?"* and *"Could you make a drone in the shape of an animal, like a dolphin?"*

With this porporsial Adamsian notion swimming, or rather soaring in his mind, the dreamer removed his robe and his nightshirt, allowing his sleeping-trousers to fall to the floor. The sudden shock of frigid air awoke his body like an electric blue shock, his skin rising in goosebumps. Like a gazelle awaking to find a hungry lion considering how best to season and sauce it for dinner, Erasmus leapt into the bathtub, slipping as his feet made contact with the smooth porcelain surface. He could make out his person in the mirror, watching in what seemed like slow-motion as his feet failed to live up to their warrant in life, their bottoms directed not towards the apartment below but to the drain at the far end of the tub. He felt the cold air rise up from the outside of his right foot through his ankle and into his calf. At his knee the slow rise of the cold porcelain up his body ceased with a hard smack upon the firm surface of the tub, his thighs and stomach slapping it as he turned his body so that he landed face down. At last he felt the worst blow as his face smacked hard upon the tub, his nose, getting the full force of the unplanned meeting with the porcelain bath. He worried that the sound of his body smacking into the tub's interior would awaken his neighbours, whether below, or on the far side of the apartment from Mel, yet to Erasmus's surprise there came no sound from the other occupants of his building on 76th Street; only the softened sound of Marie-Thérèse stirring from her packing to come check on her friend. She opened the bathroom door and found Erasmus turning over so that his back pressed down on the tub.

"Trying out for the Olympic Long Jump team?" she asked, a worried eyebrow raised.

"I was freezing, so I thought I'd jump into the shower," he replied with a groan.

"How do you feel now?" she asked, "Is anything broken?"

"I don't think so," he said, looking down at his body. He didn't see any ribs out of place, and his knees were where they were supposed to be. "But I'm even colder now," he whimpered.

She looked down at him, "I can see that."

He stopped and realised his exposed position. "Why don't you check on Mel, I have a feeling she'll be worried that we've tried to blow up the apartment with an alarm clock."

"Are you sure you don't need any help?" Marie-Thérèse responded, looking her splayed friend in the eye.

"I'll be fine. Just make sure Mel doesn't pick up detective-work again and come snooping in."

"Good thinking. You ought to turn the water on now, you'll warm yourself up faster that way," Marie-Thérèse advised, turning about quickly that the tails of her skirt flared out but a small touch, closing the lavatory door behind her.

Erasmus pushed himself over onto his knees, then grabbed hold of the side of the tub, pushing with his hands onto his feet. With his back to the shower he could make out a slight hint of blood in the bottom of the tub. He looked down again and saw that his right ankle had caught on the edge of the tub, cutting along the front near the top of the foot. Erasmus sighed, "Figures," and turned about towards the shower-head. Leaning down he turned the faucet handles, and lowered the stopper in the faucet, triggering an exertion of water from the shower-head that shocked him yet again with its frigidity. He stood there, half-frozen for a minute, waiting for the hot water to rise up to meet his battered and nigh polar corpus. With the response expected of any unextraordinary human still mildly dazed, Erasmus stood there beneath the water and let it fall atop him.

Eventually, to Erasmus's relief, and admittedly mild annoyance, after a minute Mitch Carshalton in the apartment below finished his own shower, which was the classic Carshalton twenty-minute affair,[1] allowing for the hot water to rise high enough to reach Erasmus in his shower. He cried, first in joy, and secondly in a sense that must be felt by a lobster when it is dropped in a pot of boiling water after just having its morning swim in the tank. Unlike the "individual" on the floor below, Erasmus was quick to shower, spending at most five minutes under the water. "I know how to clean myself," he said to Marie-Thérèse when she first commented on his expedient showering habits three years prior when they first shared a hotel room during a Spring Break trip to Chicago.

As he closed the taps, cutting off the flow of steamy water from the shower-head Erasmus thought of that trip. It was in March 2014, when they were both seniors at Columbia, about to finish their undergraduate degrees, Erasmus's in Computer Science, Marie-Thérèse's in Pre-Medicine and Diplomacy. *"She was always more of an over-achiever than me,"* he thought.

"I heard that," Marie-Thérèse called through the cracked-open door.

"Wait, am I thinking or talking?" Erasmus mused.

"You're talking, you always talk," she replied, peeking her head around the door.

"So, all those times when I've thought things, I've actually been whispering them?" he asked, grabbing his towel from the hook next to the tub.

"More like muttering them, you told me yourself that you cannot just think through things," she replied, pulling the door open.

"When was that?"

"You were sleepwalking at the time. After that time you brought home that bottle of vodka in honour of the anniversary of Sputnik last year."

"It's a major event in the history of computing," Erasmus replied, drying off his back by rubbing the towel back and forth up and

---

[1] Coincidentally, this is what Mel called Mitch Carshalton's excessive use of his phone to play solitaire, and what Marie-Thérèse called Mitch's frequent "house-guests", who on average would only stay for around 20 minutes and would leave with an extra $50 to $60 in their purses. "Cheap lousy ass," is the nickname that Erasmus Plumwood had for Mitch Carshalton. One is a man of deviant tastes, the other is a man of few words.

down his spine. Marie-Thérèse turned slightly away, laughing at the sudden lack of consciousness of her presence. "But I don't drink Vodka, only wine and a little cider."

"That's what you said last year, and this year on the anniversary. You get a bottle of vodka once a year, always on the anniversary of Sputnik; and every year you drink so much vodka that you forget all about it and end up sleepwalking that evening into my room pretending to be some famous Russian. Last year it was Marshal Zhukov marching into Berlin, o and my room was your Berlin," she added with a note of annoyance. "This year you were Pavlova. I bet you didn't know you could stand *en pointe*. Well, with the help of a little vodka I guess anything is possible."

"But I don't get it, I don't drink vodka!" Erasmus cried, now baffled at the thought of him *gracefully* entering Marie-Thérèse's room in ballet shoes on the tips of his toes, gracefully extending his permanently-suited-for-a-keyboard arms up above his head like the prima donna in Tchaikovsky's *Swan Lake*.

Marie-Thérèse laughed loudly enough to startle Mel out on the fire escape. "Who'll it be next year? Let me guess, someone from Pushkin, maybe from *Eugene Onegin*. I know, you'll either be Lensky or Tatiana! O, that'll be quite the sight. Will you have the letter or your best friend's bullet hole in your heart?"

"I don't know, will you be buying a gun in the next year?" Erasmus watched out the door as Marie-Thérèse walked to the kitchen where her morning tea had just concluded brewing.

"I'm Canadian, I don't need a gun like you Americans seem to. I'm friendly enough to make that unnecessary."

As Erasmus continued with his morning routine, all the while thinking about how to recreate Sputnik with a drone, Marie-Thérèse stood in the kitchen, her cup of tea in her hand. *« Je ne se compris pas, toutes les années il s'agit comme un fameux russe mais il ne sait pas des chaque russes sauf les créateurs du Spoutnik ! C'est trop bizarre pour moi ... »*[2] she thought.

Marie-Thérèse had first met Erasmus on orientation day their Freshman Year at Columbia. He was a very shy, entirely quirky introverted computer geek from Kansas City, Missouri, a city considered so provincial by the Ivy League elites who made up the majority of their class, that they hardly considered it worthy of putting on the map. Yet despite his introvertedness, and his rather unusual name, Erasmus Plumwood was a genuinely kind person. He tried to put

---

[2] "I don't understand, every year he acts like a famous Russian, but he does not know of any Russians except the creators of Sputnik! It's too bizarre for me ..."

himself out there, to go to parties, but more often than not he would leave after twenty minutes. They bonded over a love of code; Erasmus had always been fascinated with the codes that make NASA's computers run smooth enough to operate their missions to the outer Solar System, and Marie-Thérèse loved the codes that are the world's languages. She was always fascinated with learning new languages and travelling the world trying out her knowledge. A native speaker of French, she had grown up learning English from as early as she could remember, being from a bilingual city.

Her father, Louis Merlinais, worked as a sort of business liaison for the City of Montréal, and the Province of Québec as a whole, travelling all around the planet, though mostly to Europe, seeking out the best partnerships for Montréal and its native businesses. He was most proud of the work he had done with a number of vineyards in Austria's Burgenland and in the now Italian region of South Tyrol. By being the first to arrange the import of these wines that soon became best sellers throughout Québec, Louis Merlinais returned from Europe not just a liaison for his community, but a wine merchant and importer in his own right. Not only that, but that deal, made in 1998 when Marie-Thérèse was just five, was worth a whopping $100 million Canadian. *La Société de l'importation des vins environnementaux* or SIVE in short, made the Merlinais family one of the wealthiest in Canada.

It opened numerous doors for Louis, his wife Hélène, and their only daughter Marie-Thérèse that previously they could only imagine. Every year they attended the finest events in Montréal, including the annual Grand Prix in July, and had the finest seats at the Opera. When Marie-Thérèse left for Columbia in 2010, her mother Hélène Merlinais launched a second career, having stayed at home with her daughter for much of the last decade, being elected to the Québec Parliament for the Green Party in her home Riding[3] of Outremont, much to the pride of her family. With Hélène Merlinais working in Québec City, and Marie-Thérèse studying across the border in New York, Louis expanded his company's product line, from not just importing Austrian and Tyrolean wine, but also introducing French electric cars to the Québécois market. By 2013, Louis Merlinais was awarded the Order of Canada by the Governor General herself in recognition of his efforts in improving the air quality of Montréal, as his electric car imports had done so well they now represented nigh 45% of the new cars being bought in Québec. There was some discussion of whether or not his career trajectory could go any higher, though even Louis expected his fortune would not grow beyond the 2016 estimates of $50 million Canadian.

---

[3] Canadian for "constituency"

Erasmus's family was far more less successful than Marie-Thérèse's. His father was a cartographer, who had made the jump from making paper maps to digital globes for airline in-flight navigation systems in the early 2000s, just before the Recession, which put a damper on the airline industry and put Charles Plumwood out of a job. He refocused his efforts, signing a lucrative contract with the U.S. Government to help them with their mapping during the last few years of the Second Iraq War and the opening furloughs of Iraq's Civil War. His work took him from the family home in an old 1912 mansion at 58th Terrace and Wyandotte Street in Kansas City's Brookside neighbourhood about an hour and a half north every-day to Fort Leavenworth, where he worked with Army Intelligence helping them interpret their satellite images of the crisis in Iraq far below.

The military contract was a bit unacceptable for Erasmus's mother, Helvetica Burgheley Plumwood, who was decidedly anti-war, and even more fervently upset by the continued violence in Iraq, a country where she had done much of her doctoral research as a young archaeologist under the watchful eye of her mentor, Dr Humphrey Featherstone, the head of the Department of Near Eastern Archaeology at University College London. Dr Featherstone had trained his young student Helvetica Burgheley well, so well in fact she was offered a position in the Department of Near Eastern Antiquities at the British Museum upon her graduation from U.C.L. She was happy to take the position and made a name for herself as a reliable Assyriologist at the Museum, giving public lectures on how to read Cuneiform, and even offering classes on the Akkadian language to interested students who happened to pass through the museum or see her flyers stuck to lampposts around Bloomsbury.

The story that Erasmus was told by his Charles was that he had first met Helvetica on Malet Street, during a trip to London to view the cartography collections in the British Museum's Reading Room. He was intrigued in her Akkadian classes and, much to Helvetica's surprise, showed up to the one that evening. "I left with less Akkadian than I came in with," Charles would always recollect at the end of the story, "but I left with a greater appreciation for this amazing talented and intelligent woman who lived for her passions."

That Spring of 1985 Helvetica invited Charles to join her on a dig at the ancient city of Uruk in Iraq. Charles could come and help map out their finds, giving the site its first mapping in a good while. While on the trip they had to make an overnight connection in Geneva, where out of curiosity, though admittedly with some concern that she had heard this question far too many times, Charles asked Helvetica how she got her name. With a smile she looked at her now boyfriend, "My father is a bit eccentric. He named me after the image of Helvetica on the Swiss Franc coins. He used to keep a ten-centime coin in his pocket as good luck."

"So, you were named after a coin?" Charles asked, surprised but amused to know that at least she wasn't name for an entire country.

"Yes. What about you?" Helvetica is supposed to have asked.

"Well, my mother had a favourite rabbit growing up who was named for the Prince of Wales. So, my parents decided to name me Charles after her 'best friend growing up.' Only, it took a few years before my grandmother broke the news to my father that Charles wasn't a boy but a rabbit."

Marie-Thérèse always liked this story. It made her laugh. She wasn't named after a coin, or a rabbit, but after a princess, Marie-Thérèse de Bourbon, the last surviving child of Louis XVI and Marie-Antoinette; her father had always been a devoted royalist, and had even had the opportunity to meet the Queen on a trip to London with the Premier of Québec in 2006. When he was picked on by the rich pre-law students at Columbia about his name, Erasmus shouted back that he was named for the greatest humanist of the Northern Renaissance."

That frankly didn't help his image with the rich pricks, but Erasmus had grown a bit of a thick skin. He didn't really care what they thought anymore. They were never going to like him anyway. Sure, he was able to fix their computers and reset their smart watches for half the price that the professionals charged, but they never respected him. Now that graduation from their Master's degrees approached, Marie-Thérèse could sense Erasmus's excitement to get away from these Knickerbockers and their Brahmin counterparts from Boston. Now with the positive results from his phone interview with Technophilia out in San Francisco, surely Erasmus would be on his way west, to kinder waters.

With the water now finally out of his hair, Erasmus emerged, his underclothes donned beneath his robe. He briskly stepped across the corridor, his bare feet slapping on the wooden floorboards in a manner like a dead fish being slapped by the flat side of a knife blade in a fish market. Entering his room, he pushed the door closed behind him with his left heel, disrobing and crossing the room to his wardrobe once again. Erasmus opened it briskly, feeling the cold air from outside once more. "You know, you really do have some good calves. You ought to model," Mel said, sitting on the fire escape where she had been fifteen minutes prior when he left his room.

Erasmus walked to the window, his goosebumps practically visible from beneath his white underclothes, "You should turn away when someone is dressing."

"How am I to avoid watching a show when it's right here in front of me?" Mel retorted, her hands raised gesturing towards the drawn back curtains.

"Hey Mel, are the moons of Saturn still orbiting or have the rings knocked them into Jupiter?"

"That doesn't even make any sense," she replied, confused by the sarcasm in Erasmus's voice.

"I know," he curtly retorted, drawing the curtains with a brisk movement in his upper arms.

With the sudden decrease in sunlight in his room, Erasmus stumbled back in the dark to his nightstand, where he illuminated his lamp and returned around the foot of the bed to his wardrobe. Its old maple doors were opened to their owner, revealing a small collection of shirts, trousers, sweaters, suits, and coats within. Knowing how far they were travelling, and how cold it was that day both in Manhattan and in New Hampshire, Erasmus picked a collection of clothes to take with him to the White Mountains, a number of thinner shirts, some fine woollen sweaters, and a good pair of long underwear which rested on his "good calves" and thighs, offering an extra layer of warmth to keep back the cold of the Winter Sun from his pale flesh. Atop that fine cotton he drew a pair of black trousers, a fitting outer garment for someone going into a region called the White Mountains in the depths of December. The evening prior after dinner Marie-Thérèse read the forecast aloud for their packing pleasure. It was due to be nigh -23°C (-10°F) when they got to Conway, a temperature that Erasmus had only experienced on the rare occasion and Marie-Thérèse far more frequently in her youth on that island city in the Saint Lawrence River.

Finally, there was the matter of socks. Erasmus looked in his sock drawer, unsure of whether to choose the thick woolly pair or a thinner, more everyday cotton set. Remembering how the woolly socks had given him blisters the last time he wore them while walking around in Manhattan, he decided for the sake of comfort he would wear the cotton ones onto the train and change into the woolly socks when he arrived in New Hampshire.

On top he chose a yellow sweater that spoke volumes to all who observed it. Choosing to not wear a necktie this time, Erasmus let his collar come out over the top of the sweater, which came rather high and tightly over the middle of his neck. It was a style that he had seen Marie-Thérèse wear countless times, and one that he appreciated and enjoyed wearing as well, no matter how feminine it might appear to its more frequent donners. Now clothed, Erasmus stepped into his slip-on shoes that rested in their place by his bedroom door, and stepped out into the corridor, walking back towards the dining table where Marie-Thérèse sat, reading the morning paper. She looked up at her friend the coder, « Votre majesté ! » she exclaimed, smiling at him as he approached. "You look like the Sun King himself in that yellow!"

« *Merci, votre sérénissime !* » he replied, bowing gracefully yet with a wry grin on his face. "You know, this is the first time since my alarm went off that you've seen me clothed."

"You know, I had noticed your lack of garments for a while there. Are you trying out nudism now?"

"Only on Sunday mornings."

"Fitting. I'm sure Monsignor Calazzi approves."

"I doubt it, but I know Mel appreciates it."

"Mel appreciates anyone who comes closer to their cosmic nature."

"You bet I do!" came the cry from the fire escape.

Erasmus looked towards the window in his room, "Don't you ever have to go inside and pee?"

"Nah, that's what this litre bottle is for!"

Erasmus turned back to Marie-Thérèse, blushing, "I thought that was an off-brand liquor."

Marie-Thérèse rolled her eyes, then motioned behind her to the kitchen, "Are you going to eat anything? We have a long day ahead of us."

Erasmus walked past Marie-Thérèse's seat, affirming her question and going for the bread box. He withdrew a package of crumpets that he had bought at one of the local British stores. Crumpets were a favourite of his mother's, and now of his, from his earliest years when they lived just off Great Portland Street in London. Dropping a pair in the toaster, he activated the appliance with a downward push of the black lever, whose dark colour reflected in the stainless steel of its main body. Stepping away from the toaster for nigh a minute Erasmus opened the sauce cupboard and pulled out his favourite Canadian maple syrup, before taking the three steps behind him and to his right to the fridge, where he withdrew a jar of French strawberry preserves. With his usual allotted 45 seconds now elapsed, Erasmus returned to the toaster and flipped the lever to its more frequent elevated position. He turned to the cutlery drawer and gingerly so as not to disturb its fellows, withdrew a small fork that he used to pierce the crumpet, pulling it out of the toaster so that he did not burn his fingers. He then realised he hadn't chosen a plate to put the crumpet onto, and leaned to this left over the counter to a cupboard in the corner where the plates and bowls were kept. Opening the cupboard with his left hand, the right presently occupied holding a fork that dangled a toasted crumpet, he reached in and sinisterly selected a small plate upon which to some relief he let the crumpet drop. Returning to the toaster, Erasmus took hold of the second crumpet, which sat in the leftmost toasting drop, removing it from its place of warmth and restoring its place with its fellow atop his plate.

Taking the jam in hand, Erasmus returned to the cutlery drawer in front of him, withdrawing it and choosing a butter knife to spread the preserves with atop his crumpets. Then, once they were properly jammed, the breakfaster poured a healthy pond of maple syrup atop the plate, drenching his crumpets like a Chicago cook baptises an Italian beef sandwich in its own juice. Taking the fork and knife from the countertop into his right hand, and the plate with its precious cargo of jammed crumpets baptised in Canada's finest maple syrup in his dominant left hand Erasmus turned about and walked to the dining table, setting the plate down in his normal place next to Marie-Thérèse, who looked on at it with her usual sense of bemusement.

"You eat that every day, why not change things every once in a while?" she asked, setting down her newspaper for a moment.

"I find it relaxing to eat the same thing every day. Plus, these remind me of my mother."

Erasmus returned to the kitchen and poured himself some hot water from the electric kettle on the counter, choosing an English breakfast teabag from their tea box to drink that morning. Returning to the table, the teacup delicately held by his left fingertips as its handle was far too small to hold the handle any more firmly, Erasmus set it down onto its saucer, which he had held in his right hand, never having mastered the art of carrying a hot teacup by its saucer alone, something which his grandfather Burgheley, a former civil servant in the Ministry for Transport, always said proved he was more American than English.

Erasmus was more than ready to eat his breakfast, as he was on most days. His parents had instilled in him a strict custom of never eating prior to a.) the morning teethbrushing and b.) showering and dressing. Erasmus had always kept up with this tradition, and saw it as something to be admired, something that wasn't just civilised but was also healthy. He yearned to impress his English grandparents, who were tried and true old imperialists. His grandfather had followed in the footsteps of his father, Sir Cecil Burgheley, who had worked as a civil servant, first for Lloyd-George in the Ministry of Munitions during the First World War, and later in the Home Office. Both Sir Cecil and Erasmus's grandfather Arthur had been members of the Reform Club in their day; both were ardent Liberals, and though they never stood for election to the House of Commons, were nevertheless highly regarded by the leaders and MPs of the Liberal Party and its successor the Liberal Democrats since then young Cecil Burgheley had built such a strong relationship with Britain's last Liberal Prime Minister, the Welsh Wizard David Lloyd-George. In taking his first few bites of his pair of crumpets each morning, Erasmus was reminded of the roots of his family, of his mother Helvetica the Assyriologist, his grandfather Arthur the eccentric civil servant, and his great-grandfather whose work in the civil service a century prior to Erasmus's breakfast now just beginning had helped the British Empire win the First World War, out supplying the Germans and their allies.

Though not out rightly thinking about Kaiser Wilhelm as he ate a bit of crumpet, Erasmus nevertheless did think about how he wanted to have a couple of German sausages, preferably Klabsbratwürste when he was next by his favourite German deli on 57th Street. Come to think of it, Jackson, New Hampshire isn't too far from Berlin, New Hampshire. *"Maybe, we can go up there and see if they have any good Currywurst."*

"They don't have Currywurst in Berlin, New Hampshire," Marie-Thérèse said not looking away from her paper, "most of the people in Berlin are Québécois."

"And how do the Germans feel about that?" Erasmus retorted, annoyed that he had been merely thinking aloud since at least 2010.

"I don't think the Germans know or care about what goes on in Berlin, New Hampshire."

"Even though it's named for their capital?"

"Do you think people in Columbus, Ohio care what goes on in Columbus, Kansas?" she asked, folding and dropping her newspaper on the table.

"How do you know there's a Columbus, Kansas?"

"You muttered it when you were thinking about going to your cousin Monica's house for cards when you were going back to Kansas City in October."

"Damn it, M.T.!"

Marie-Thérèse chuckled, rising from her chair and taking her now emptied cheese plate back to the kitchen sink to wash it and return it to its home safe, sound, and dark in the cupboard above the countertop. Erasmus returned to his crumpets, tickling their honeycombs with the tines of his fork as he looked for the best place to stab into the soft, buttery, jammed, and syruped delicacy so to import as much as possible into his mouth in as expedient a manner as possible, considering Marie-Thérèse had risen from breakfast and would soon want them to be on their way down to Penn Station.

It was going to be a long day of travelling, nigh over eight hours, but thankfully with only one transfer in Portland, Maine, unless one included the walk from the subway at 34th and 7th Avenue to the intercity platforms in Penn Station proper. Quickly finishing off the second crumpet, Erasmus jumped up from his seat, washed off the plate with a finesse that would make any health inspector proud,[4] and set himself to the task of packing what little he had left to attend to. Returning to Mel's favourite domestic TV comedy, he brought his suitcase atop his bed and opened wide its mouth, checking to make sure everything that he needed lay within. He had spent the better part of

---

[4] Except the real jerks.

Saturday evening, before his interview with Bruce Tybald at Technophilia, neatly folding and packing the most essential winter clothes and paraphernalia into his sleek dark green suitcase. The bright red luggage tag that spent its life strapped onto the suitcase's top handle made Monsignor Calazzi proud, who took it as Erasmus's expression of his pride in his *fictitious* Italian heritage.

Now as their 08:15 departure from Penn Station approached, Erasmus hurried his pace like a rushed performance of the *Hurrian Hymn*, throwing a couple of last minute socks into the top of his suitcase, letting the lid flop closed like a farmyard gate dropped onto its side, slamming shut with the aid of Earth's gravitational pull, firmly though not entirely in line with the main frame of his suitcase below. Erasmus reset the lid with his right hand, while zipping the gravitationally-enthralled element of the bag firmly to the rest of the case. With his suitcase packed, and ready to go, Erasmus turned about, grabbing it by its top handle, and let it drop to the floor, its weight making a pronounced thud[5] as it made contact with the hardwood below. Erasmus could scarcely make out the sound of Mitch Carshalton waking with a start at the sound in the room below him. Like most mornings Erasmus could hear what sounded like an arm falling across an abdomen in its first morning wakings. Who was it last night, the coder thought as he dragged his bag across the floor into the corridor.

Marie-Thérèse stood waiting in the corridor, her suitcase already well packed, a backpack strapped over her shoulders, weighed down by a day's worth of snacks and other supplies for the journey north. "Are you ready to go," she asked impatiently glancing at her wristwatch.

"Yes, I think so," Erasmus replied.

"Alright then," Marie-Thérèse placed a blue tam with white trimmings atop her head, allowing its sides to extend in all directions, offering her face some added protection from the occasional snowflake or gust of wind, "I think we should be going."

Marie-Thérèse turned, her grey overcoat elegantly turning with her person. She took five steps forward and opened their front door, exposing the somewhat subdued aura of the hall beyond to the electric light of their apartment's main corridor. The light from within began to soak into the darkness of the hall, pushing it into full retreat for a good two or three doors on either side of their apartment. Marie-Thérèse walked out into the hall, leaving their door agape for Erasmus to follow on. He made his way towards the doorway, stopping just briefly at their coat closet to extract his dark green overcoat from within. It was warm and cosy, reminding Erasmus of the bed that he had

---

[5] T. H. U. D., pronounced thud.

abandoned so abruptly just an hour before. How amazingly soft and fine those sheets and blanket were, yet still the adventure before them filled Erasmus with a sense of excited anticipation.

Erasmus stepped out of the apartment, a pang of resentment emanating from his suitcase which never quite cared for the threshold it had to cross every time its owner put it to task carrying his clothes, shoes, and other essential goods on a long trip. Thankfully for his suitcase, Erasmus wasn't going west to Kansas City this time, so it wouldn't have quite as long of a journey in the air with its fellows of all sizes soaring inland from the Atlantic coast towards that garden city at the confluence of two mighty rivers. No, this time Erasmus's suitcase might well have wished to remain safely, warmly, stowed beneath his bed as it would be travelling to a far more frigid place, up in the northern reaches of that spinal ridge that crossed down the heart of New England.

Without much immediate regard for the feelings of his suitcase, which hardly registered as a discernible concern for the coder, considering even his conception of reality left little room for luggage sentimentality, Erasmus followed Marie-Thérèse along their corridor and down the stairs that led to the front of their building on 76th Street three storeys below. Whether or not it had any sentiment or sense of its surroundings, Erasmus's suitcase nevertheless was a heavy load to lug down to the ground floor. Knowing he would have to carry it with him into the subway and back out again once they reached Penn Station, Erasmus resigned himself to accept the fact that he had much to learn in the art of packing.

In contrast, Marie-Thérèse was swift in descending the flights, her suitcase, while bulky as all suitcases are, nevertheless glided along above each step with ease, her blue knee-high suede riding boots clicking along each step with a refined thud as they descended per their wearer's volition from the elevated quarters of their domestic habitation to the cold, wind-battered pavement beyond the building's elegant edifice. At the bottom of the stairs, Marie-Thérèse turned, ensuring Erasmus was close on her heels. He looked at her with a sense of relief at reaching the bottom of the stair, setting his suitcase wheels-down on the floor and extending its handle upwards, that he could pull it ahead to the subway five blocks away. Holding open the door, Marie-Thérèse pulled it agape with a determination that challenged the winter air beyond like Patroclus defying Hector's superior swordsmanship by donning the armour of Achilles. Marie-Thérèse was by no means an Amazonian conqueror of the wrathful rays of the Winter Sun, despite being from one of the coldest cities in the Americas. While she bared Erasmus and herself to the frigid air, she nevertheless shuddered at the sudden shock of borelian breath that rushed across her face. Erasmus could well see the cold air slam into Marie-Thérèse's skin, and subconsciously began to prepare for the worst that winter could offer.

Marie-Thérèse stepped out from the lobby and looked up into the sky. Above the bare branches of the trees a pale blue sky, fainter than in Summer, echoed the curved rays of the Winer Sun down onto the Earth, its rays hardly strong enough upon impact to fully extend the solar warmth they had initially embodied, instead echoing the cold heart of the north wind as the shell echoes the beat of the *cipín* on the goatskin face of a *bodhrán*. Like the drumbeat of the *bodhrán* too, Erasmus's heart leapt in concern at just what its mind was getting it into. Sure enough, with a few quick strides, Erasmus was likewise out in the cold winter air, an air considered so cruel by many that not even toddlers or bears would dare leave their hovels to face its wicked wrath.

In the face of this hemispheric frigidarium, Erasmus and Marie-Thérèse stepped outdoors, rising up to the sidewalk level from their slightly lowered front door meagerly and cold to see a city silent with the frost, yet thankfully yet without much snow. they walked side by side westwards down the sidewalk to Amsterdam Avenue where they turned left, heading south past still shuttered businesses, their owners stirring towards the same locale as the two travellers at that moment, preparing for what they expected would be another busy Sunday of holiday shopping ahead. At 72nd Street the pair crossed Amsterdam Avenue to Verdi Square, where at Broadway's southeastwardly curving they descended into the Subway, going through the turnstiles with only the slightest complexity having both lived in Manhattan now for the better part of the last six years.

At Penn Station Marie-Thérèse and Erasmus once again raised their suitcases up, lifting them up the stairway that led from the subway platform down another corridor and through a large atrium to track 18.

At the top of the stairs leading down to track 18 stood a ticket collector, whose job had drifted slightly from the original intent of its title, as he no longer *collected* tickets but rather inspected and scanned them to ensure they were with the correct passenger. The ticket collector took Marie-Thérèse's and Erasmus's tickets in hand, each in its own turn, and inspected them thoroughly. With everything seemingly in order, having come up as belonging to the correct people, the ticket collector began to wave them on. Yet suddenly an unannounced beep sounded from his scanner. Looking down, the ticket collector immediately took in a sharp breath. He looked back up at the pair, "Which one of you is not an American citizen?" he asked curtly.

"That's me, sir," Marie-Thérèse replied, used now to the question.

"I need to see your passport. There's a new directive from Washington. All foreigners must show their passports before boarding domestic trains or busses in the United States," he held out his hand to receive the blue leather binding emblazoned with the Royal Arms of Canada.

The ticket collector took the passport and gave it a quick look over. "You are from Quebec, I take it?"

"Yes, sir," Marie-Thérèse replied.

"How long have you been in the United States?"

"I have lived here for the past six years, sir."

"Where have you been living?"

"Here in New York, sir. I am a student at Columbia," Marie-Thérèse replied, a hint of irritation beginning to wax in her voice.

"Alright, off you go, Madame Merlinaise," the ticket collector said, handing Marie-Thérèse back her passport.

"Thank you, sir," she replied, quickly taking it in hand and proceeding down the stairs to the platform below.

Erasmus was taken aback at what he had just seen. Nevertheless, the ticket collector seemed pleased with Marie-Thérèse's responses. Erasmus clutched his suitcase and descended down the old stairs, an endangered relic of the great cathedral of a station that once stood on that site.

Erasmus caught up to Marie-Thérèse, "Why didn't you correct him?"

"Carriage 10, ah, here it is," Marie-Thérèse thought aloud, finding their carriage and stepping aboard.

Erasmus followed her steps onto the train, and down into the rows to their seats near the centre of the carriage. They took their seats next to each other, the darkness of the Penn Station tunnels beneath Manhattan seeming to hide the ghosts of travellers past in their darkened surfaces.

Now seated, Erasmus looked at his friend, her face seemed somewhat pale. "Why —"

"Why didn't I correct that guard?" Marie-Thérèse finished his thought, "Because today it's not always safe to be an immigrant here in the United States. This country was founded by immigrants, built up by immigrants; hell, even these tunnels were dug by immigrants. Yet now this country's government seems to believe immigrants are like rats and need to be eradicated from their cities for the sake of public health and safety."

"But so many immigrants work for the rich, for the bigwigs in Washington, and here in New York," Erasmus tristefully argued, hearing the sense of anger and shock flow through Marie-Thérèse's voice, her fair skin pale as if she had seen one of the tunnel ghosts that had carved through the metamorphic rock that lay beneath the surface of Manhattan.

"Yes, yet the powerful still need poorer people, native born Americans, to vote for them to keep them in power. They need a scapegoat to distract attention from the harm their business interests are causing to ordinary people like you and me. So, they make immigrants one of the enemies. There are similar people back in Canada, but my mother has fought very hard to keep them from gaining influence in the Québec Parliament."

"So some people are fighting back," Erasmus replied optimistically.

"Yes, some are, but not enough have a voice to counter these fearmongers."

As they spoke the last of the passengers boarded their train, and the doors slid closed. "Good morning, for those of you just joining us this is Anne your conductor speaking. This is the 8:15 departure from New York Penn Station, a continuing service from Washington, D.C.. Our final destination is Portland, Maine. We will be stopping at New Rochelle, New York; Stamford, Connecticut; Bridgeport, Connecticut; New Haven, Connecticut; New London, Connecticut; Mystic, Connecticut; Westerly, Rhode Island; Kingston, Rhode Island; Providence, Rhode Island; Westwood, Massachusetts; Boston-Back Bay, Massachusetts; Boston-South Station, Massachusetts; Portsmouth, New Hampshire; and Portland, Maine. Customers wishing to travel to Hartford, Springfield, or Vermont should leave this train at New Haven."

"We've got a long way to go..." Erasmus thought, listening to the list of stations they'd be calling at on their way to Maine.

He looked over at Marie-Thérèse and found her removing her travel necessities from the front pocket of her suitcase. Out came a book, one that Erasmus had seen around the apartment, *Les rêves des chiens*. Erasmus figured it must be a book about loping through fields chasing cats, rabbits, and hens, but he had been mistaken before about Marie-Thérèse's reading habits, so for all he knew it could be a book romanticising the Isle of Dogs in the old London Docklands. What romance could be found there today, except the odd office fling? Then again, perhaps this book was a comedy, set in one of Erasmus's favourite London neighbourhood names: Mudchute.

Marie-Thérèse continued extracting a collection of paraphernalia from her suitcase. *"How the hell did she fit a ham and cheese sandwich in there?"* Erasmus thought, amazed at the lunches she had packed for the pair of them.

Astounded at all that he was seeing, Erasmus failed to notice that the train had begun to move. Soon they were speeding through the East River tunnels and heading in a northeastwardly direction towards

Connecticut. As they crossed Long Island, Erasmus could feel the weight of his exhaustion fall upon his eyes. He really had been busy that morning, and certainly hadn't gotten enough sleep the night before. How many hours had it been? Five? Six? He couldn't recall. Regardless, his eyelids were growing profounder by the minute, as if weighed down by an excessive application of force.

Soon all was still, the rumble of the train being the only sound that registered in his mind. Erasmus found himself lying in some wet grass, surely not far from where he last was. He raised his head and looked about, *"this didn't look like New York... they don't build houses like that there."*

Erasmus propped himself up with his forearms, *"Ooo look, a rabbit!"* he thought with a burst of sudden excitement.

The rabbit ran in the opposite direction from Erasmus who, with an eagerness known to the most exuberant of souls, amongst which Erasmus did not consider himself company, Erasmus bounded up onto his feet and chased the rabbit across the grass to a fence where it slipped through, avoiding his grasp by a mere hair. Erasmus looked mournfully at the rabbit through the fence, *"I just wanted to say hello!"*

"Look at the Portuguese Water Dog!" a woman's voice shouted from nearby.

Erasmus turned to look. He had always appreciated dogs, but hadn't ever seen a Portuguese Water Dog before. There were no dogs behind him, just a couple of young women who were in their late twenties. They looked as though they came from somewhere in India originally, their faces beamed with delight at seeing a *Portuguese Water Dog*, whatever that was. *"But where's this dog? Now I'm confused,"* Erasmus thought.

He walked about the grass for a minute, mentally establishing that this grass was inside a park of some sort. After a minute he found himself leaving the grass, walking onto a footpath that crossed the centre of the park. Along the footpath was an old wrought iron bench, dating back at least fifty if not sixty years. Erasmus strolled up to the bench, and in the act of mounting it to sit upon it he noticed a puddle in front of the bench, a puddle that he was standing squarely in. *"Damnit,"* he thought at the sudden wetness of his feet.

"Wait a minute, why am I barefoot?"

Erasmus looked down into the puddle and was startled by the reflection of the dog looking back at him. *"What the hell?!"*

"Why do they call it a Portuguese Water Dog?" one of the women asked the other from a few metres away.

"I'm not sure, but they say that Port—" Erasmus felt a hand push on his shoulder. His eyes opened to the bright light of day reflecting off of a snowy bay to his right.

"It's about time that you woke up," Marie-Thérèse said, "We're almost to Portland."

"O good," Erasmus replied wearily. He must have slept for about three and a half hours, after all these new 200 mile per hour trains make good time going up and down the Atlantic coast. He looked out the window and saw the snow-covered fields and hills of Maine, a new state for him. "It looks cold out there."

"Yeah, the conductor said it's around -12°C in Portland right now.

"O boy," Erasmus replied, thinking hard as to where his thick woollen overcoat had ended up. As they neared the train's final destination, he remembered it was on the shelf above him. *"What a relief,"* he thought, sitting back into his seat and preparing for the coming chill.

3

"Jackson and Quincy"

-12°C! Erasmus remembered those January nights in Kansas City where the wailing northwesterly winds howled such a frigid temperature, which has picked up speed hurling itself southeast across the Great Plains from the High Rockies in Wyoming and Montana. He could well recall that sort of climate but felt no yearning for it in his heart. Nevertheless, Erasmus looked about the carriage and could immediately make out the locals, the hearty New Englanders for whom this was a constant normality in their far northern homeland.

Marie-Thérèse sat next to Erasmus, waiting for her companion to rise from his seat and alight from the train carriage. He was taking a tad longer than normal, fumbling about with his things, his hands beginning to shiver with the cold air that had swept through the now opened carriage doors like a spectral phantom of winters past. "Erasmus, we need to get going," she asserted.

"I know," Erasmus replied, looking bleakly at the seat in front of him.

"What's wrong?"

"I forgot my mittens."

"O no –"

"They were made from kittens."

"What?"

"And with them I was smitten."

"Erasmus, you're rhyming now."

"Am I not a poet?"

"You wouldn't know it."

"Perhaps it's time to show it ..."

"Do you want to go for it?"

"For what?" Erasmus replied, an eyebrow raised with an air of slap-happiness.

"Go for the next train that we have to catch," Marie-Thérèse retorted with a wolf's smile.

"How long do we have?"

"Twenty minutes."

"That's not terribly long."

"No, but if you don't move I'll sing you a song."

Erasmus rose from his seat, collected his suitcase from the overhead shelf where he had placed it, and walked down the length of the carriage to its rear door, where he descended the step to the concrete platform below. Sure as he expected, the cold air swirled about his face, consuming it in a frozen embrace like the nimble arms of death itself, raised from its petrified tomb by the song of the Northern Cardinal, its wistful air swirling in pitch with the resonance of the piercing boreal zephyr through the resting bare branches of the trees, naked in their sleep in such a climate as this within which they could not sustain their vital means as in the warmer months of Summer. Erasmus stepped forward on the platform, disembarking from the train fully and looking about. "Do you know which platform our next train is at?" he called back to Marie-Thérèse, her blue tam standing out against the stark whiteness of the snowy landscape around them, itself contrasting the deep blue of the afternoon Winter sky.

"It says Platform 3," Marie-Thérèse replied, looking up at a departure board above them.

"Platform 3 it is then," Erasmus responded, walking toward a staircase that led up to the overhead concourse connecting the station's four platforms. The cold air permeated all corners of the station, as it was built to largely be open air. Only in the 1960s had the now defunct New England Railroad made a concerted effort to install sliding doors between the concourse and the departures hall, where row upon row of passengers waited shivering cold in the winter months without any artificial heat to keep them warm in those long cold months. Passing the seductive warmth of the departures hall, whose doors slid open and shut again at the companions' passing, Marie-Thérèse and Erasmus took the stairs down from the concourse onto Platforms 3 and 4, which they found abandoned of any locomotive or carriages. Even the rats that were accustomed to scouring for their daily bread amidst the tracks, scampering to and fro to secure that little morsel of food that may have been dropped by a passing traveller, railway worker, or station staff, were hidden away beneath the tracks in their burrows, where the wind could not scrape away at their fur or skin.

"It should be here at any minute, yes?" Marie-Thérèse muttered.

"I think so," Erasmus replied, checking his phone for their travel information. It was already past three in the afternoon. The train bound for New Hampshire was due to leave Portland in just ten minutes. "Where do you suppose this train is? This is its first stop."

"It's probably still in the shed being readied by the crew," Marie-Thérèse replied, while texting something quickly on her phone through her high-tech gloves that allowed her to type on a touch screen while wearing them.

"*Fair point,*" Erasmus thought. Unlike his Canadian friend he was well and truly frozen to the bone. He hadn't planned to be this cold before fully arriving in New Hampshire. All of his warmest clothes were safely packed away in his suitcase. "*Should I take out an extra sweater and put that on?*" he thought – "*No, the train'll be here in ten minutes at most, there's not enough time to do that." – "It's too damn cold!"*

"How are you staying so warm?" Erasmus asked Marie-Thérèse, who had replaced her phone into her pocket.

"I'm wearing enough layers that the cold doesn't bother me as much. Where are you the coldest?"

Erasmus thought for a moment, "Well, my face feels like it's being stabbed by a dozen ice picks sharpened by the finest Spanish swordsmith in Toledo, I can hardly feel my hands, my legs and toes are frozen stiff by this breeze, and my ears are searing red."

"Well, you need to wear a hat that'll block some of the wind from your face and ears. You already said you forgot your mittens, which I have to say I was looking forward to seeing. I mean, who doesn't love mittens with kittens on them? Now the trick to keeping your legs warm are a good pair of leggings, but your masculinity would hardly allow for that, now would it?"

"If it keeps me warm, why should I ignore a good idea?"

Marie-Thérèse nodded in agreement. She had planned well for the cold, having grown up so used to it in Montréal's unbeatable winters. Her blue knee-high suede riding boots kept much of the wind out from her feet, ankles, and calves. Her legs were well encased in a pair of thicker tights that were almost leggings, certainly providing enough warmth for her. Her upper body was well wrapped in a couple of shirts, with a good thick cashmere sweater atop those for added warmth. Now that they were off the train she had redonned her heavier winter overcoat, which went down to the knee and flared out at the waist. Its woollen fabric was a good material to keep the wind out and her body warmth in. Her face was sheltered by the crescendoing bonnet of her blue tam, which blocked a good deal of the wind from above her head. Nevertheless, she wore a fine woollen scarf about her neck, allowing it to rise up and block some air from reaching her face from below. Thus, while her face remained uncovered, she nevertheless felt protected from being "benumb'd with hard Frosts" as Purcell described it in *The Fairy Queen*.

Erasmus looked beyond the station, towards the trees that lined the far side of the parking lot. They seemed far hardier than he, more accustomed to this seasonal cold that came each year only to leave again partway through the next. *"What's it like to live in such a cold climate?"* he thought, his feet dancing slightly with the cold air around him. The air continued to swirl, driven forth from the northwest by a strong breeze. Erasmus clutched the lapels of his overcoat, pulling them together, left over right, hoping beyond hope that he could usher in a renewed sense of warmth within his body.

A few more minutes passed before the train pulled into Portland station, coming up alongside Platform 3 with the smoothness of a fine twenty-first century machine, a wonder of the modern age. The old clacking of the train on the tracks was well since past, only a train bell remained to sound the engine and carriages' arrival in Maine's largest city. "That's it," Marie-Thérèse said, returning her phone to her pocket and looking ahead at the slowing carriages. As the café car came alongside the companions, the rush of air emitted from the force of the train pushed a lock of Marie-Thérèse's bangs out of place and in front of her left eye. She quickly restored the brunette strands to their place, descending from within her tam with a certain degree of aid from the planet's gravity. Collecting her suitcase in hand, she led Erasmus up to the train doors. These slower regional trains did not have seat assignments, unlike the faster national services, giving Marie-Thérèse and Erasmus more liberty to decide how they would board the train for New Hampshire. It filled Erasmus with a sense of relief, akin to the glowing joys of a nice cup of *chocolat* that they could leave the frozen air of Portland sooner rather than later and board the train at its nearest door.

Watching as the train doors glided open on their rails, Marie-Thérèse could hardly make it on board before the shivering wreck of a Missourian behind her darted past her through the door and into the carriage. He was not well suited to the cold, despite coming from an English family. His mother, Helvetica, had always asserted that she had chosen to study the Ancient Assyrians out of an absolute detestation for the cold. Her father would often retort that "cold air makes for strong bones," to which Helvetica always replied, "As long as my bones are strong enough to study dead bones, I'm fine with my skeletal health."

Erasmus often wondered about the eccentricities of his family. Were they the result of some predetermination by a higher being, someone out there who devised their entire life's stories? Perhaps they were bored and dreamed up a quirky family with a rather exciting set of lives? Perhaps that being was as bored as someone flying transatlantic in economy class, though Erasmus doubted that any higher power could be that bored, otherwise they'd have forced the mere mortals who run the airlines to make their services more enjoyable. *"Whomever it was must have had a great sense of humour though,"* he thought. *"a humourless nimb couldn't have created beings like us."*

On board, Erasmus and Marie-Thérèse found their way to a set of table seats. She quickly stowed her things above them on the overhead shelf, an action which he quickly imitated with great vigour, the firm desire to take a seat and speed across the Maine countryside to Conway, New Hampshire. The border between the two, though well set since colonial times was increasingly fluid with the shift to and fro of jobs and opportunities between the two states. The peoples of these two states moved across it with relative ease, *"not unlike frozen custard out of the custard-maker,"* Erasmus thought, dreaming the slightly warmer climate of Kansas City and the joys of frozen custard, so duly loved across the Midwest. "Vanilla with banana bites, brownies, and cookie dough," he muttered wistfully.

"Dreaming of dessert again?" Marie-Thérèse asked, a smile as wry as Athena's curving her cheeks with the air of one who knew more than she needed, but one who really didn't mind.

"Only the finest," Erasmus sighed, turning to his friend and gazing dreamily into her eyes.

"You can dance your words about as much as you want, you're not getting even a morsel of frozen custard in this weather."

"No, but I can envisage it, deep down in the recesses of my mind. What's wrong about dreaming of home?"

"Nothing, except that when I'm not there it makes me sad."

"Do you miss your family, M.T.?" Erasmus asked, his brows lowered in soft arches that matched the dolorous tone of his voice.

« Toujours. »

"Why don't you go back to Montréal, surely there are jobs up there?"

"There are, but I want a city of my own, not just the place where everyone knows my parents. Can you imagine living in their shadows?"

Erasmus thought about it, his parents didn't put off much of a shadow, being nigh higher than 5 feet tall. "That depends on what sort of shadow you mean."

"O," Marie-Thérèse picked up on the comment, "damnit, Erasmus! I'm close to crying and you're making short jokes!"

"I'm sorry, M.T., the punchlines are just too abrupt to ignore."

"You'll be a punchline if you keep this up," came a voice from behind them.

Erasmus turned about, peering between the seats. There sat a woman, small in stature yet as grand a personality as any. "I'm sorry, ma'am," he called over his shoulder.

"You'd better be!" she cried back, reaching to kick his seat in disgust only to miss it by a few centimetres.

The P.A. system activated, announcing the conductor's gentle voice, "Good afternoon, and welcome aboard this service calling at Casco, Bridgton, and Fryeburg in Maine, Conway, Gorham, Jefferson, and Lancaster in New Hampshire, St. Johnsbury, Danville, Marshfield, Plainfield, and Montpelier in Vermont. We are now departing Portland, Maine. Customers for Jefferson, N.H. should sit in the front three carriages, as that station has a short platform."

"Wait, does this train go by Jackson, N.H.?" Erasmus asked.

"Yes," Marie-Thérèse confirmed, "but it doesn't stop there. Conway is closer than Gorham, plus it has a rental car office."

"Ah, okay," Erasmus assented, leaning back in his seat. He looked dreamily out at the snowy white landscape beyond the warmth of the train. The window itself was cold, a breath of air cringing its way from the glass onto Erasmus's face. He leaned to the right slightly, hoping to better distance himself from the sharpness of that frigid air. Resting his body up against the warmer right-hand-side of his seat he felt a sudden sharp pain in his back. *"I must have leaned the wrong way!"* he thought at that sudden burst of spinal consciousness. The blow came a second time, a piercing shot directly into his back. "What the hell was that?" he asked. Marie-Thérèse looked up from her book, catching his concerned look. They turned about, perceiving from between their seats the woman behind them, thrusting her umbrella like Don Quixote's lance into the belly of Erasmus's seat.

"Ma'am, do you mind?" Erasmus asked, wary of what response her lips might utter.

"Do I mind?! No, I don't mind being insulted by some man! Lady, you should be ashamed to know this guy!" she shouted to Marie-Thérèse.

"I'll have you know, he's really a nice guy. Please, *madame*, leave us alone."

The woman looked even more indignant at being called *madame*, "What do you think I am, lady?"

Marie-Thérèse realized her mistake quickly, sighing audibly at the miscommunication. "Ma'am, I'm sorry if I spoke out of turn to you. We never meant to offend you, honestly."

"Well, what would you foreigners know about American culture? You can offend me with even the smallest words!"

The conductor came down the aisle, her warm winter coat draped over her left arm. She stopped next to the woman's row, "Is there a problem here?"

"Yes, these two have been making fun of me!" the woman screamed.

The conductor turned to Marie-Thérèse and Erasmus, "Is this true?"

"Ma'am, we were laughing about my parents."

"O sure!" the woman snorted.

"Honestly, ma'am, we never meant to offend her."

"Yeah, well why'd you call me a whore then?"

The conductor was taken aback by this, "I didn't hear anything about that—" she said

"That one," the woman shouted, pointing at Marie-Thérèse, "the foreigner called me a madam."

Marie-Thérèse turned in her seat, standing to face the woman, who became even more indignant at seeing her insulter look her in the eye. Marie-Thérèse turned to the conductor, "*Madame*, I did not intend to call this woman any name, just to show her we meant no disrespect."

"Where are you from?" the conductor asked.

"Montréal."

The conductor took one more look at the three passengers before her. She turned to the woman, "Ma'am, this train is not full. If you'd like I can reseat you."

"No, they should be thrown off the train! They're foreigners!"

"Ma'am, please keep your voice down," the conductor replied, in an authoritative but smooth tone.

"Why don't you throw them off the train?"

"Because they haven't done anything wrong. Now, ma'am, if you could come with me. I will seat you in a different carriage where you won't have to sit near them."

"Fine, but I want my money back. This trip is costing me a fortune!"

The woman rose from her seat and stormed down the aisle, leaving her belongings behind her. The conductor quickly gathered what she could and followed the woman down the train and into the next carriage. Marie-Thérèse sighed, sliding back down into her seat. "What the hell!" she muttered

"Some people are just very touchy," Erasmus replied, putting a hand on Marie-Thérèse's arm to comfort her.

They sat in silence for a few minutes, listening to the train fly past little hamlets and villages, whose denizens were wont to be about on such a cold winter's day. The sky out their window was a baby blue, yet sharp as the daggers of ice that hung from the roofs of the houses and churches that they passed. "Is this what Québec looks like in winter?" Erasmus asked.

"It's similar, especially when you're near the coast."

"I've never seen so much snow."

"Doesn't it snow a lot in Kansas City?"

"It used to. One winter about four years ago it snowed nearly a meter in two days, but that's very rare."

The conductor returned, walking down the aisle with determination, her black leather boots making a defined marching sound at her presence, like the suffragettes of a century prior. She stopped at Marie-Thérèse's and Erasmus's row. "I want to apologize for that scene, you shouldn't have had to deal with that," she said with regret in her voice.

"Is everything alright?" Marie-Thérèse asked.

"Yes. She's been moved to a different carriage. I informed her that she had violated the rules of conduct aboard a national service train, and that she would be asked to leave the train at the next station if she had a similar outburst again."

"Wow," Erasmus goffed incredulously.

"Are you both alright?"

"Yes, we're fine."

"Where are you travelling to?"

"Conway."

"Ah, alright. Well, we'll be there shortly. Again, my apologies for the disturbance, and please have a pleasant journey."

The conductor turned to leave them, heading towards the front of the train again where she could begin her regular task to checking tickets.

"She was one in a million," Erasmus said.

"Yes, maybe she was just having a bad day."

"Quite possibly. Who knows what was happening in her life, but I hope she's feeling happier now."

The friends looked at each other, catching one another's eyes. Erasmus hadn't realized how deeply brown Marie-Thérèse's were, yet the clearness of that brown made him feel all the happier to be in her company.

Marie-Thérèse looked back at her friend, whose gaze reminded her of another friend she once knew, back in Montréal. She smiled, happy to be with Erasmus on this journey into the white snowscape of New Hampshire.

They passed through Casco and Bridgton, stopping just before the border in Fryeburg. The degree to which the forests in this region remained intact, despite centuries of lumbering astounded Erasmus.

The forests seemed to be masters of this region, their mighty trees rising high over the little roads and lanes beneath their branches. Not even four centuries of colonization, settlement, and industry could vanquish the mighty northern forests that populated these mountains. The high branches watched over the people who dwelt below, their arms hosting many a wild creature at a safe enough distance from the forest floor so to keep them safe from harm.

Erasmus watched as the forest began to disappear before him, and the first signs of the town of Conway came into view. It was like any other small New England town, built in the colonial period and developed with the introduction of industrial logging and tourism in the nineteenth century. This railway had helped make the town the centre of the White Mountains that it had become. English colonists had settled Conway, yet Conway today was very American. The train passed by little houses and shops, each with their own character, purpose, and design; the train's glass and metal carriages making quite the unique sight amidst the wood and stone of the town. The church steeples rose above the rooftops crowning Conway with their ecclesiastical glory. This was a land far removed from the skyscrapers of the cities, whose towering heights could be seen only on the townspeople's televisions and in their memories of adventures and past lives in Boston and New York. This was the America that Washington Irving and Nathaniel Hawthorne had written about, the America of *Our Town* and Bedford Falls. A truly small-town America, one that both Marie-Thérèse and Erasmus were unfamiliar with.

Both came from cities, Erasmus from Kansas City's leafy Crestwood neighbourhood, once a stagecoach stop south of the city proper on the far side of Brush Creek in a valley where the old streetcar line ran along the road a small brook long since covered over by a fine boulevard. Marie-Thérèse came from a far older, more established city, one whose gleaming glass towers matched the history of its old French heart in their prominence and esteem. Both Marie-Thérèse and Erasmus had passed through small towns like this, whether they be Dubuque or Mont-Tremblant, yet neither of them had spent any significant amount of time in such a place. Now they felt the train begin to slow as it approached Conway Station, the platforms long enough to fit the old intercity trains that came north direct from New York, bringing tourists with them from that great city to the mountain ski slopes of New Hampshire.

The P.A. system rang into life again, "This is Conway, New Hampshire. Please be sure you have all your belongings before leaving the train."

The train came to a defining halt along the main platform at Conway Station, just a few short steps from the station house. The life of the station seemed congregated elsewhere, as save for the handful of passengers leaving the train there, no one else was on the platform. Erasmus rose from his seat, following Marie-Thérèse down the aisle, their suitcases in their hands, and to the train door. Marie-Thérèse descended gingerly, unsure if there was ice on the concrete platform below the door. She let the toes of her boots make the first contact with the soil of New Hampshire, before lowering her heels onto the platform as well. Stepping out three paces from the train, and moving to the left, Marie-Thérèse turned about to watch Erasmus follow her path down from the train onto the platform. He had a slightly harder time, having taken a more intrepid approach of jumping down from the train, giving his knees a run for their money with the sudden increase in kinetic energy from his rapid descent onto the platform. Erasmus winced in pain as his knees popped at that unannounced blow to their integrity, yet the pain was brief, hardly worth noticing except for the small layer of slush on the platform where his feet landed, causing their landing to become more of a backwards fall, like an unfortunate whale descending from a great height. Marie-Thérèse acted instinctively, stepping towards Erasmus, cognizant of the slush on the platform, and reaching out to grab his hand. Seeing only a blur of pale blue and a fair hand in stark resolution, Erasmus reached out and grabbed the palm before him. His eyes returned to normal focus, the panic of falling beneath the train now subsided, yet he quickly realized he had only just missed hitting his head on the adjacent carriage, which itself was a mere 30 seconds from leaving the station on its journey northwards to Gorham.

"Lift me up, please!" Erasmus cried, scared of what could happen if the train left with his head so close to its side.

Marie-Thérèse pulled, her upper body workouts now paying off threefold. Erasmus was able to regain some composure, and sturdying his feet on the ground he helped Marie-Thérèse help him, raising himself up to a standing position. "You should be a gymnast," Erasmus said, regaining his proper posture and brushing off his coat. Luckily his hat had remained in its coronal place, nesting atop his head with an air of dumbfounded resilience to the forces of gravity.

"And you should be in the ballet," Marie-Thérèse replied, "that was quite spectacular of you."

"Well, I do my best."

"Just promise me one thing," she replied, collecting her suitcase and watching as Erasmus picked up his from the ground, "Don't end up in a morgue while we're on this trip."

"Why not? The coffin ought to be cheaper here!"

"Erasmus!"

"What? They don't have sales tax in New Hampshire. Everything ought to be cheaper here."

Marie-Thérèse shook her head in disbelief at her friend's dismissive jestering of her concern for his wellbeing.

Their suitcases in hand, and hats firmly positioned atop their heads, Erasmus walked the six paces forwards into the station house. Marie-Thérèse, still bemused by his unconcerned view of mortality, followed after a moment, pulling open the great wooden door, whose large glass window presented a hall that had seen many a traveller from near and far since its construction in the late 19th century. Its Victorian architecture used deep, dark local woods, from trees that were felled by the lumberjacks of five generations prior–

"It's Second Empire architecture, what are you talking about?" Marie-Thérèse thought to herself.

Sorry, may I continue?

"Yes, just keep your architectural styles straight. C'est narrateur n'est pas faible ! »[6]

Anyway, its **Second Empire** architecture used deep, dark local woods, from trees that were felled by the lumberjacks of five generations prior. Those trees, despite their departures from their maiden forests, nevertheless retained a sense of their spirit, here

---

[6] "This narrator isn't reliable!"

enshrined in a grand structure alongside their fellows. The station house was still very much the working heart of the regional train and bus network, but it nevertheless was home to some small exhibits on the local railway history. There were old daguerreotypes of great old trees being chopped down by lumberjacks, and of the iron horses of yore steaming their way north and west from Boston, New York, and Portland.

There were photos of local men going off to fight against the Kaiser in 1917 and against the Nazis in 1941, leaving from this very station on their long journey across the wild Atlantic. There were images of nurses from the local hospital waiting for soldiers who were returning home, many from France, and some from the South Pacific, wounded but not yet beaten, their courage insurmountable. There was an image of Calvin Coolidge coming north to Conway, while serving as President, for a brief vacation away from the stress and strain of Washington. The town shown in its history and vibrancy through these displays, it's life and memory living behind these cases, where surely, Marie-Thérèse thought, some local grandmother or grandfather would often take their grandchildren to see what life was like here in Conway in their day.

"Which way d'ya think is the rental car place?" Erasmus asked, looking out towards the parking lot on the side opposite of the station from the platforms.

Marie-Thérèse looked up from the local history cases. "I'm not sure." She looked around, gazing out of the windows that overlooked the quarter-full parking lot beyond. After a moment she saw a sign, "It looks like there's a rental car place over there, to the right," she pointed, her right arm extended, drawing her right index finger out like that of a patriotic Marianne calling *tous les français* to arms. She stepped forward, with a martial air in her pace, walking with a purpose out of the door and towards the northmost parking lot, where, by her estimates, the rental cars were available. What could be said of the air of magnificence with which she took her person out of the station and towards that parking lot? Erasmus mused on this subject for a moment, determining that if any air was to be taken from this action it was that the air outside the station house was colder than all the souls in Hell if they sighed in a unison chorus like a dog emitting a half sigh, half snort in its sleep on a heatless winter's night.

He pushed open the great front door of the station, felt the breeze brush against his cheeks, and quickly left the station building, heading for the parking lot where Marie-Thérèse was already talking with a man who seemed to be the rental car agent. As he walked in their direction, Erasmus saw the agent point to an SUV two rows back in the lot. Marie-Thérèse picked her suitcase up from the ground and walked towards it, her feet crunching in a layer of snow, perhaps 1.5 cm deep at most. The snow had fallen earlier that morning, before dawn when the valley was its coolest, when most of its residents were still safely and warmly nestled in their beds. The cold winds blowing down off of the mountains, from high above the peak of Mount Washington whose tempestuous winds challenged even the boldest climbers at all times of the year. Erasmus waited for a small white hatchback to pass in front of him before crossing the street that ran between the station house and the parking lots. The hatchback's engine spluttered as it passed, backfiring with such a ruckus that heads turned in the herds of deer a mile away in the coniferous woods on the mountainside.

"Gunshot!" the white-speckled deer cried.

"What where?" its fellow with a light brown coat asked.

"Down there, in the valley."

"Near the town?"

"Yeah. I think so," the white-speckled deer replied.

"Are you sure it wasn't up here in the trees?"

"Is everyone here?"

"Let's see," the light brown-coated deer replied. He turned his muscular neck to the right and to the left, walking four paces forward down the hill to see if anyone was behind the boulder nearby. "Yes, I think the herd is here."

"Good," the white-speckled deer sighed in relief, lowering her head to take a bite of some of the undergrowth.

"Don't worry too much though. It's winter. Plus, the humans have started shooting each other more lately than us."

"O, why?" the white-speckled deer asked, raising her head in uncertainty and fear.

"Sheer stupidity? Do I look like an expert in humans?" retorted the light brown-coated deer incredulously.

"Humans are strange animals," the white-speckled deer replied, turning and walking up the mountainside to look for something more to eat on the low-hanging branches of the trees.

Far below the deer, Erasmus walked into the parking lot, and passing the parking attendant with a hearty, "Hello, " he walked up to Marie-Thérèse who was loading her suitcase into the back of the Japanese made SUV that the agent had rented out to them for the journey. "Did your Dad import this one too?" Erasmus asked jokingly.

"No. He just imports French cars into Québec. The American government hasn't given approval for their import in to the U.S. just yet," Marie-Thérèse replied, taking Erasmus's suitcase from his hands and placing it up in the back of the SUV next to hers.

Marie-Thérèse pressed a button on the car's remote control, closing the back door with the smoothness of an automated sliding window shade. Erasmus turned his head to her, asking as they watched the door lower to a close, "So, do you want to drive?"

"Sure. Do you mind?"

"No, not at all."

Erasmus crossed past Marie-Thérèse, turning left to walk up to the front passenger side door, while the Montréalaise returned to the driver's door opposite Erasmus. As they climbed up into the car, both clicked the heels of their footwear, her boots and his shoes, displacing any snow that had built up on their heels and soles as they had walked a good hundred meters in that light snow, albeit with a tad bit more slush on the station platform when they first descended from the train, Marie-Thérèse more thoughtfully, Erasmus more instinctively and thus dramatically. Their heels cleaner, they both swung their legs into the car, Marie-Thérèse's skirts flaring out a tad more than those of Erasmus's coat, whose heavier woollen fabric kept it more stationary when moving at pace. Marie-Thérèse was the first to close her door, surprising Erasmus who expected her to put her seatbelt on first, having seen her do things in that order the time she came with him to visit his family in Kansas City. He thought about commenting on it, but decided it was too trivial a discrepancy to acknowledge aloud.

"Aren't you cold?" Marie-Thérèse asked, noticing Erasmus was sitting there, his door still ajar.

"O yeah, whoops," Erasmus muttered, acknowledging his situation after a moment's lapse into deep thought.

"Are you okay? Did you hurt yourself at all on the platform?"

"I'm okay, just thinking."

"Okay," Marie-Thérèse replied, unsure if "just thinking" was a positive or a negative in this instance.

Turning back to the dashboard in front of her, Marie-Thérèse put the key into the ignition, turning it and letting the engine burst into life. She waited a few moments for it to flare up in revolutions before calming back down again before putting the car into gear and pulling away from the parking spot. Turning left, she drove down the lane before taking another right and cruising out of the parking lot.

Marie-Thérèse guided the car to the left once onto the street, past the station before taking a right at the next cross street that ran alongside a strip mall until she came to a stop at a red light where the side street met the White Mountain Highway. As she drove, Erasmus pulled out a map of New Hampshire that was in the glovebox. There was Conway, along U.S. Highway 302, aka the White Mountain Highway, at the intersection with State Highway 16, just west of the Maine border. He followed the White Mountain Highway northward with his finger, "It looks like we take this until Glen where State Highway 16 breaks off and keeps going north," he said, directing Marie-Thérèse as best he could.

"So, should I turn left here?" she asked, the opposing traffic lights now turning orange, about to become a bright shade of red.

"Yes," Erasmus replied, lowering the map and looking up at the intersection before them.

Their light turned green, and Marie-Thérèse released the break, exerting pressure on the gas instead. The SUV advanced into the intersection, turning left with the direction of the driver at the wheel before heading northwards through town. To their right was a nice little five-and-dime store, like so many others that had since disappeared across the U.S. and Canada. Just beyond that a toyshop, its wooden guards announcing the playfulness of its occupants. To the left they passed a number of small local shops, each advertising its own unique brands of products. On the right again just passed Mechanic Street was the library, a place that had they not wanted to get to their inn would certainly have been a stop for the travellers.

Past the library they came to a school for mountaineers, said to be one of the finest along the Atlantic coast. Further ahead were a variety of ski related shops and a large hotel that catered to the skiing public. As the White Mountain Highway began to turn they passed a white church whose small bell-steeple rose above the neighbouring buildings with a poise reserved for houses of worship alone. Beyond the church they began to make their way through the outskirts of town, passing by small houses and the occasional shop, gas station, and market. Heading further north, the highway came closer to the Saco River, whose course it followed near Conway town.

As the road continued to curve this way and that they passed between woods and forests, past lodges, inns, and old farmhouses some of which had seen generation after generation pass by on this road since colonial times. Crossing the East Branch of the Saco River on a bridge near the village of Bartlett they passed by a number of local tourist attractions that had been well visited by children over the past half-century, their toy soldiers, play slides, and fun parks all showing their age, yet equally the fun to be had there. "Do you want to stop at one of these fun parks?" Erasmus asked.

"When I was six, I tried to play with some other children on a small merry-go-round type circular platform that they were spinning around, but there were too many children on it and I was knocked over. My legs were stuck underneath it."

"Ouch!"

"And the worse part about it was that the other children didn't stop spinning it, and the adults wouldn't help me either."

"What did you do?" Erasmus asked.

"I screamed until someone came over and stopped it spinning."

"How bad was it?"

"My legs were pretty badly cut up, but nothing more than that. Still, I think I'll avoid the fun parks from here on out."

"Yeah, I don't blame you for wanting to skip out on those after that. That sounds awful!"

They drove another couple of minutes in silence, until they came to the fork in the road where the White Mountain Highway left State Highway 16 and headed west. "Alright, you'll want to turn right here," Erasmus said, pointing at where State Highway 16 left the larger road. They made the turn with ease, aided by the curved turn lanes that were built with the first appearance of cars in these mountains at the turn of the twentieth century.

"So, I have a question for you, Erasmus."

"What is it?" he asked, turning his head to look at Marie-Thérèse, who continued to face forward at the road before them.

"Do you care that I'm driving and not you?"

"What do you mean?" Erasmus asked, a scent of what she was getting at resting in his mind, yet unsure if that was the right train of thought.

"Well, some men don't like it when women drive; they want to drive themselves," she explained.

"O," noted Erasmus, confirming his suspicion. "No, I don't mind at all. You're a good driver. What more is there to say?"

"Nothing. I'm just curious."

"Look, Marie-Thérèse," Erasmus said, his eyes trained on her soft pale face, "you may be a woman, and a beautiful one at that," a demi-smile quickly appeared on her face, "but as far as I'm concerned that has no effect on your abilities as a person. You're just as capable of doing what you do well as any other person. The fact that you're a woman has no bearing on your abilities as a driver. All that matters there is that you're a good, observant driver."

Marie-Thérèse's smile became far more pronounced now. « Merci, Erasmus. Tu es sympa, »[7] she replied, blushing slightly.

— « De rien, mais tu n'as pas une chose de moi à remercier, c'est la vérité. »[8]

They continued driving northward along State Highway 16, a renewed sense of comradery existing between the friends, who both thought to themselves how happy they had come on this trip together, and how happy they were to get away from the bustle and madness of New York for a week. Erasmus felt confident that he would know where to turn next and let the map rest unread in his lap. He knew they'd come across the covered bridge that marked the entrance into the village of Jackson itself, but he wasn't entirely sure where it would be.

---

[7] "Thank you, Erasmus. You're a nice person."

[8] "You're welcome, but you have nothing to thank, it's the truth."

Erasmus thought about that name, Jackson. The village was surely named for Andrew Jackson, the President famous for winning the Battle of New Orleans, conquering Spanish Florida for the United States, and instigating one of the greatest crimes against humanity against the Native Americans that any European American leader would ever directly order. Yet here was a village, in the northern marches of New Hampshire that was named for that fiery-tempered President from Tennessee. *"Why didn't they name it after a prominent New Englander of the day like Daniel Webster or John Quincy Adams?"* he thought, *"Quincy, New Hampshire. Now there's a nice name."*

Erasmus had always liked John Quincy Adams. The son of patriots who had given their all to the cause of American independence during the Revolution, he had served as a Lawyer, Ambassador, President, and Congressman during his long career of public service stretching from his younger years in the 1780s until his death in the 1840s. Erasmus even remembered once seeing a photograph of Quincy Adams, the first President to ever be photographed. Granted, he wasn't in office when the image was captured, but nevertheless he was the first holder of the office of President of the United States whose image was captured through the scientific wonder of photography.

A deer off in the trees to the left of the road caught Erasmus's eye, and he turned his head to follow it as it ran off up the hillside away from the road. Unsure of why it seemed so interesting to him, Erasmus restored himself to his normal neck position, facing forward and watching the road ahead. A river flowed alongside them on the right. *"Surely soon we'll see the covered bridge that leads into Jackson,"* he thought.

They continued northward, following the course of the river for a good while further, crossing it on a more regular modern road bridge, near a large local restaurant that seemed like a good place to get a burger. Driving still further northward, they followed the river into White Mountain National Forest. As they entered the National Forest and began to rise in elevation, the highway began to pick up in speed, its wide turning banks rising out of the rock on terraced shelves carved into the mountainsides. Erasmus noticed a trailhead leading off to a waterfall, "Winniweta Falls," he read aloud from the large brown National Forest Service sign.

"That must be neat to visit in the summer," Marie-Thérèse replied, glancing briefly at the sign before resuming her view of the road before them.

They continued on their way, curving this way and that up further into the mountains. Erasmus was beginning to be worried, "Do you think we missed our turn?"

Marie-Thérèse shot her eyes at him, "You're the one with the map."

Erasmus paused for a moment. "Alright, let me know which mile marker you see next," he replied, figuring that if he could figure out where on the highway they were he could then determine if they were close to Jackson yet.

Marie-Thérèse looked out, but it seemed there weren't any mile markers anywhere around them. She continued at full-speed, climbing ever higher alongside the high mountain valley that the highway followed. With each passing curve Erasmus was ever surer they had missed their turn. "Did you see a covered bridge back there at all?" he asked, dread filling his voice.

Marie-Thérèse thought for a moment. "Yes, a few kilometres back, along that river."

"Damnit!" Erasmus cried, realizing he must have missed the turn off into Jackson when he saw the deer. "Turn around!"

"Just a minute, I need to find a safe spot," Marie-Thérèse replied, her tone becoming less gentle and more severe, largely in response to Erasmus's sudden outburst.

They drove on for another minute, until Erasmus saw what looked like a good turnaround point, "Over there, to your right. That looks safe enough!" Erasmus pointed to the side of the road where the drop off into the valley was further removed from the roadside.

"Okay," Marie-Thérèse replied, turning the wheel and sliding the car into position. The ground was covered in a deeper layer of freshly fallen snow, the clouds having just burnt up in the early afternoon Sun. Marie-Thérèse pushed hard down on the breaks, but the SUV still slid further than she had wanted towards the barrier fence in front of them that marked the northern end of that turn off area. She held onto the wheel, knuckles white with trepidation at going off the cliff edge and into the valley far below. The car came to a halt, but only just in time. Marie-Thérèse and Erasmus sighed with relief, looking at each other, their mutual admiration having lessened slightly with their tense exchange of words prior to the car's stopping.

Erasmus looked out the windows as Marie-Thérèse thought how best to turn around.

"Maybe if I put the car into reverse, I can back up enough to have room to change gear back to drive and turn this around to go south again," she thought, eyeballing the drop off in front of her.

"Marie-Thérèse–"

"Not now."

"M.T., look–"

"What?" she asked, distracting herself from her three-point-turn planning for a moment to see what Henry the Navigator had been distracted by this time.

Erasmus pointed into the valley, opening his door and stepping out onto the soft snowy ground. He stared down for a long moment, "What is it, Erasmus!?" she shouted, the wind howling along the highway down the valley.

"A waterfall!" he cried, turning to face her, a big broad smile from ear to ear spreading wide across his face.

4

Falling

The waterfall seemed serenely thawed amidst the snow and icepack of the valley and mountains surrounding it. The rush of flowing water heading down the valley towards its junction with the Saco to the south. The current was rushing towards its tumultuous descent beneath the snowpack, surely melting the snow and thus alleviating the degree to which the valley would become inundated with the white stuff during the colder months. "It's so beautiful," Marie-Thérèse said, stepping across the front of the car and towards the cliff edge. She peered down into the chasm, in awe of the wonderous waterfall below.

"Have you ever seen anything quite like it?" Erasmus asked.

"Once, in the Rockies, but nothing quite like this here in the Northeast."

Erasmus looked down into the chasm towards the falls below. His oft hibernating sense of adventure unrestrained by caution for once. He turned, looking at Marie-Thérèse with a grin on his face. She looked back at him, a lack of assurance and an air of uncertainty spread across hers. "Do you want to go down there?" he asked.

"What're you thinking of?"

"Well, I'm up for a little adventure."

"O, come on now, who do you think you are?"

"I feel like a Bilbo for once."

"Erasmus –"

"No, c'mon, M.T., it'll be fun!"

"Climbing down a cliff to a waterfall in this weather?" she asked, looking up into the sky at the still falling snow.

"Well, if you don't want to climb we could always fly down there."

"Erasmus, Bilbo didn't have wings."

"Fair point," he noted, looking down again, trying to judge just how far the fall would be.

Marie-Thérèse turned about, looking across the highway to see how the steady flow of cars, semis, trucks, and vans was progressing, if they could easily turn around at that point on the highway. She noticed a trailhead directly across from them, catching her breath at the thought of Erasmus seeing the same marker that could guide him towards his dream of climbing down into the valley to see this waterfall.

"O, look! There's a trailhead over there!" he shouted, pointing at it from across the highway.

« *Merde !* » Marie-Thérèse muttered under her breath, really not wanting to have to climb down a valley in this weather. Sure, many a Québécoise before her had travelled over worse ground in winter, but she wasn't inclined to do any sort of voyageuring on that Sunday.

Erasmus started to walk over towards it. "C'mon, Marie-Thérèse! This'll be fun!"

As he turned to continue on his way, his right shoe became dislodged from his foot, refusing to take another step forward in the now deeper snow that went up to his shins. The snowbank was only rising higher, a result of the snowploughs forcing the fallen powder off of the highway for the safety of passing motorists. "Erasmus, wait!" Marie-Thérèse called after him, like a teacher to a student far too eager to play with the soon-to-be dissected frogs in biology class. "You'll need better shoes if you're going to do this."

Erasmus looked down, his right foot now quite thoroughly chilled in the snow. "What do you suggest?"

Marie-Thérèse walked to the trunk, pressing the button on the remote and letting it glide up and open. "I brought an extra pair of snow boots, figuring that you'd forget yours."

"You're smart."

"I know. Now get over here and put these boots on."

Erasmus looked at the snow boots, they went up to the knee, and were well laced in front. Their lining looked made out of a thick fabric, maybe wool, though probably not fur, as Marie-Thérèse and her mother, the Green Party MP, wouldn't approve. "Where'd you get those?" Erasmus asked, stepping forward and taking the right boot in hand.

"The women's section at that big department store on 4th Avenue."

"Are you sure they'll fit me?" he asked, pulling the right boot up over his ankle and calf.

"I think you'll be surprised."

To his astonishment it fit like a glove. Erasmus began lacing the boot up, ensuring that neither its internal warmth nor his foot would escape and go flying out into the valley below. Erasmus paused for a moment, thinking of the best way to tie the laces into a knot at the top of the boot so they would stay in place. He thought of the photos of Tenzing and Hillary climbing to the top of Everest back in the '50s.

His grandfather had the cover photo from that issue of his favourite Fleet Street broadsheet cut out and framed, placed in a position of honour on his living room wall. Old Arthur Burgheley had apparently once met Sir Edmund Hillary, when the famed mountaineer was visiting the Natural History Museum in South Kensington to give a talk about his journey up to the highest reaches of the Earth's surface. Arthur, then a young civil servant just graduated from Oxford, was far more eager to not only hear Sir Edmund talk, but also to meet the hero from New Zealand. After the talk finished, as Arthur told the story, "I slipped a note in between two constables and ensured it ended up in Hillary's possession. Two days later I received a letter, thanking me for my interest and wishing me well in my career with the ministry."

Erasmus smiled at the thought of his grandfather, a fine old English gentleman who he hadn't seen in four years. His grandfather had died a man proud of what he'd accomplished in life. Erasmus remembered arriving at his house after the funeral at the new St Pancras along Euston Road. The old family's townhouse on the eastern side of Russell Square was the last private residence in that row, as so many of the other families that had lived there in decades past had since been replaced in their homes with a variety of businessmen, solicitors, barristers, and departments and faculties of the University of London whose Senate House towered over Bloomsbury like a giant monolith from a grander time in those waning years of the Empire. The Burgheley family had lived at No. 42 since Erasmus's second great-grandfather Erasmus Burgheley, named for his distant great-uncle Erasmus Darwin, bought the place in the 1880s after making his name and earning enough to live comfortably from his work with the Midland Railway at the nearby St Pancras Station, whose gothic spires and arches rose high above the neighbouring streets and lanes like a cathedral to the newly invented wonders of Britain's industrial heart.

The house was full of mementos from generations of his mother's family. There were letters, diplomas, and certificates recognising decades of public service undertaken by the Burgheleys, from a commendation from the Director of the British Museum at Helvetica's work in uncovering new cuneiform tablets in the ancient libraries lying desolate beneath the shifting sands of Iraq to the certificate attesting to her grandfather's knighthood, signed by George V in 1919 as the horrors of the First World War began to pass from the present into memory for millions around the globe. In a back closet they even found some of the elder Erasmus's suits, left unworn and on their hangers for almost eighty years since the elder Erasmus's death at the time of the Abdication Crisis. The younger Erasmus remembered his grandfather's stories about the elder Erasmus, a fine old Victorian who had known Gladstone during his third and fourth premierships, when the papers raved with fear of the Liberal PM's supposed aim to abolish the House of Lords. The elder Erasmus was, like so many of his descendants, an avid adventurer, who enjoyed fondly hiking through the Scottish Highlands, and even on one occasion walked out of the family's front door on Russell Square, only to walk south to the Seven Sisters Beach outside of Brighton, a full 100 kilometres away. It took him two days, but he accomplished what he set out to do. "Columbus discovered the New World, and Drake sailed the *Golden Hind* from one end of the Earth to the other, but I'm well and happy with exploring Surrey and Sussex," he said to his wife and children upon his return.

The younger Erasmus smiled, remembering these stories of his well-travelled and adventurous ancestors. He took off his left shoe, replacing it with the boot to match the one already laced up his right leg. Marie-Thérèse meanwhile was inspecting the massed snow pile along the side of the highway, looking for a good place to cross it where the snow wouldn't be too deep. As warm as her attire was, she was sure her legwear wouldn't stay warm once inundated by the over-the-knee-high snow that awaited them. Erasmus watched from his position sitting in the back of the SUV, his back resting against their stored suitcases.

Marie-Thérèse tested the snow depth, sticking her foot deep into the snow at a point a few metres to the south of the car. "I think this'll be the best place to cross," she shouted back over the wind.

"How deep is it there?" Erasmus shouted back, leaning slightly to the right to see past the car.

"Only up to my knee," came the reply.

"O, only!" Erasmus shouted back, his calls repulsed by the rising wind along the highway. A large semi barrelled down from the north towards them, passing at high speed.

"Erasmus, are you sure this is a good idea?" Marie-Thérèse shouted, real fear emanating in her voice.

"We just need to time it right to avoid the vehicles," he replied, walking over from the SUV, whose back door began to glide shut at his departure, towards his friend along the back side of the snow pile.

As Erasmus restored his place at Marie-Thérèse's side, she took another step forward, beginning the process of traversing the snow pile that only seemed to get bigger the further she went through it. "My legs are freezing!"

"I thought you liked the cold?"

"I'm fine with it, but this is something entirely different!" she cried back, the warmth draining from her legs with each passing step.

Erasmus followed after her, careful this time to stay in her footsteps. His boots were quite well tied, refusing admission to any flake of snow that attempted to pierce their warm, protective shell about his legs and feet. Nevertheless, he was taken aback at how hard Marie-Thérèse was struggling to make it through the snow pile to the highway beyond. A terrifying flash of thought ran through Erasmus's mind, of Marie-Thérèse making it through the snow pile and letting her body rest for a moment while standing on the side of the highway only to be suddenly obliterated by a passing lumber truck. He looked ahead at his friend, who was now ever closer to the highway, "Be careful, Marie-Thérèse!" he shouted.

She turned her head, while still struggling with the snow about her feet and legs, "No kidding, Erasmus!"

Marie-Thérèse cleared the snow pile, reaching the highway beyond without the grace and poise that she normally had in her footsteps. Erasmus saw her standing there, along the side of the highway, watching the passing traffic with a keen eye. He returned his thoughts to her footsteps, taking his time to make it from one to the next, each foot proceeding in a delicate yet necessary motion towards the clear pavement of the highway ahead. With another three steps, Erasmus joined Marie-Thérèse at that point, their leg muscles now fully awake at the sharp motions which they had been required to make in their last few paces.

"What're you thinking?" Erasmus asked, panting heavily.

"I think we need to judge this well," she replied, "see how the traffic is coming around a curve in the highway just ahead there?" Marie-Thérèse pointed ahead, "we need to figure out how to know what's coming around that bend and when."

"Can we hear them coming?" Erasmus asked.

"Good point, and it's getting closer to sunset, so let's look for their shadows as they round that bend."

They watched for a minute as various minivans, cars, and trucks passed. "It seems like there must be a traffic light up there somewhere, or something that's keeping them from all coming at once," Erasmus noted, his eyes fixed on the vehicles.

"When I say go, we run. Got it?" Marie-Thérèse commanded, her voice sharper, the wind certainly throwing daggers into her face.

"Gotcha," Erasmus replied, like a soldier acknowledging a superior officer.

Marie-Thérèse watched as a red minivan drove past them, seemingly at a slower speed than was necessary.

"C'mon, c'mon, go the speed limit!" Erasmus muttered.

The minivan cleared their place. "Okay, go!" Marie-Thérèse shouted, like a commandant leading a group of revolutionaries in a charge on a government barracks in revolutionary St. Petersburg or Berlin.

They ran at speed, their boots impeding them from reaching any greater feats of swiftness. Erasmus was slower than Marie-Thérèse, he less used to the boots that she had so graciously given to him for the day. As they crossed the northbound lanes everything seemed fine, yet once they made it across the double yellow median they suddenly saw a large truck carrying a heavy load of minerals southbound. The driver hit his breaks, laying on his horn as the friends ran in front of him, crossing the highway with a good 15 seconds to spare before the truck reached them. Its driver sped up at the clearing of the coast and was soon out of sight.

"That was terrifying!" Marie-Thérèse shouted, the two of them now off the concrete and standing on the forest's undergrowth. The trees were still a few metres away, yet they nevertheless their presence dominated the scene.

"Look, there's a sign," Erasmus called, pointing ahead of them southwards were a large National Forest Service sign displayed in bold black letters "GLEN ELLIS FALLS".

"Glen Ellis Falls," Marie-Thérèse read, following Erasmus towards the sign.

Erasmus reached it and stopped. "It looks like we take the foot-tunnel under the highway to some stairs that will take us down there.

"Okay. Hey, Erasmus, what time is it?"

Erasmus hadn't thought of the time for a while. He pulled back his right sleeve and looked at his watch. "It's three o'clock," he noted, "why?"

"I think sunset here is around 4:00," she replied, noticing for the first time the Sun beginning to lower towards the mountaintops above them.

"Well, we'd better hurry," Erasmus replied, smiling and taking the first steps down towards the tunnel.

Marie-Thérèse followed him, eyeing this tunnel with some uncertainty. It was little more than a large corrugated metal halfpipe inverted and sealed in place by a thick layer of concrete that made the base of the highway above. "Are you sure this is safe?"

Erasmus stopped and peered into the tunnel, "No, though most of the smaller creatures that might live in her in the Summer are probably hibernating right now."

"True," Marie-Thérèse commented, "there's something eerie about this place."

"Don't worry about it, let's go through!" Erasmus called back, the wind now far less bold that they were below the level of the highway. He walked through the tunnel, looking to right and left at the graffiti left by the many hikers and adventurers who came before them. There were many hearts engraved with the initials of couples who had ventured here, some dated to St. Valentine's, others perhaps marking anniversaries. *"Maybe I should carve a heart with the initials M.T. & F, in honour of Marie-Thérèse's reunion with Fear when she saw this tunnel?"* he thought, *"No. That's not nice."*

Erasmus turned about to see Marie-Thérèse following him, "C'mon, let's get to the stairs," he said, waving to her.

"There are so many love stories here," she said, looking at the hearts, "So many stories for a little tunnel."

Marie-Thérèse followed Erasmus out of the tunnel's far side and to a landing at the top of a long stairway. They looked over the wooden railing, "Listen to that! Those birds!" Marie-Thérèse cried, "There are winter birds down here."

"It must be warmer in this little hideaway than up above."

Marie-Thérèse began to walk down the stairs, her eyes on the steps as each one came, her mind and heart on the birdsong that she could hear echoing from below along the river. Erasmus watched on from the landing, as his friend descended cautiously down the stair, each foot leaving a mark before the last one in the snow covering the way.

"I guess she isn't scared anymore," Erasmus muttered, his mouth only slightly opening to express the words to the air.

He followed, taking each step one at a time down the stairs, carved out of the rock of the valley wall by engineers a century prior. He always found himself thinking of Theodore Roosevelt whenever he was in a National Park or a National Forest. The environmentalist President, T.R. had been the instigator of the system of federal parks and forests that dotted the American landscape. The wooden railings that lined the stairway were sturdy enough to offer Erasmus a sense of ease and security that he wouldn't tumble down into the icepack below, ending his brief life right then and there. As he walked further downward, he came to the second landing, where the stair turned a bit to the right to follow the side of the cliff rock out of which it was hewn. After a few more minutes of descending, struggling in places to not slip and fall, he reached one of the lower landings, where the stair turned again, heading more directly toward the sound of rushing water. At this point he had not seen Marie-Thérèse for some time and was beginning to be concerned that she might have fallen. But even the locals could hear Holmes and Moriarty fall from the Reichenbach, so surely, he too would have heard if his friend had lost her step and landed below.

As he turned a final corner he saw Marie-Thérèse standing ahead of him, staring at the birds nestled in the trees at the water's edge. The falls were slightly muted by the thick cover of snow and ice, and only the bottom two metres of water could properly be seen falling from the river's height. "Isn't it wonderful?!" Marie-Thérèse asked, the jubilation of a five-year-old in her voice, "Such wonderful things!"

Erasmus stepped up next to her, looking at the rushing water before them, "It's beautiful," an oasis of life in deep winter.

Erasmus held out his arm, placing it around Marie-Thérèse's shoulders and giving her a warm embrace. She smiled, "It really is cold out here."

Erasmus laughed, "Yeah, I could use a cup of *chocolat* right now.

They stared at the falls for a minute, both mentally acknowledging that they'd never really hugged before. It was unfamiliar, yet pleasant to experience.

"I'm happy we came, M.T.," Erasmus whispered.

"Me too," she replied, leaning her head onto his shoulder.

"I could stay here and listen to these birds forever," he sighed.

The birds sang their sweet song together, two northern cardinals nestled together in the tree. Their radiant plumage radiated against the white of the snow about their home. Erasmus turned to Marie-Thérèse, his eyes gazing into hers, "Will you dance with me?"

"I'd love to," she said, stepping back a pace.

They bowed to each other, and taking her left hand in his right, placing his left hand on her waist, they waltzed together, allowing the birdsong to transform into a melody as smooth and nostalgic as any by Liszt or Strauss. As they danced together all the world beyond their little oasis in the mountains vanished, the traffic on the highway far above them, the innkeeper who was surely expecting their arrival further downstream, the bustle of Conway and the madness of New York, all was gone now. Only they, Erasmus and Marie-Thérèse remained, best friends as they knew themselves to be, no matter how little they acknowledged it.

Their eyes and smiles met, locking onto each other with all the power of their emotional bond. And even as the cardinals flew away from their nest, confounded by the dancing humans below, Marie-Thérèse and Erasmus continued in their soft, intimate waltz there on the snow next to the waterfall. A few minutes passed and they retreated from each other's arms, bowing respectably before coming together again with a warm kiss and a deep hug. « *Tu es tellement belle,* »[9] Erasmus said, returning from their kiss.

« *Je pense que je t'aime, Erasmus Plumwood,* » Marie-Thérèse whispered back.

They stepped back from each other's arms, and stared into each other's eyes, the admission of what each had thought might be possible for these past years finally being expressed. Erasmus looked into her eyes, the trepidation that had in past come with such a topic beginning to tremble up his arms, "I, I love you too, Marie-Thérèse," he stammered.

It was a scary phrase to say, yet as soon as he said it her smile became even greater, she leaned up to him and kissed him again, their lips embracing as their bodies had only a few moments before.

Erasmus whispered into her ear, "Does this mean we're a couple?"

"I suppose so," she replied, whispering back.

"I feel like I'm falling," Erasmus sighed, "but I don't mind."

---

[9] "You are so beautiful"

"Are you falling into my arms?" Marie-Thérèse laughed, stepping back a pace and staring at her boyfriend.

"What better place is there to fall into?"

Marie-Thérèse came closer, taking Erasmus's hand, "We'd better be going. The Sun's about to go beneath the mountains, and there's the innkeeper waiting for us in Jackson."

Erasmus smiled, "Alright then, let's be off."

They climbed back up the stairs, Marie-Thérèse once more leading the way. The climb up was far more difficult than the descent down. She let go of Erasmus' hand when they reached the railing, taking hold of it and letting it guide her upwards towards the tunnel. As they ascended it seemed that time had slowed to a crawl. The stillness of the air near the base of the waterfall was steadily being replaced by the brisk rushing air of the highway above them. Erasmus followed on, always two steps below her as he would on an escalator. They reached the tunnel, both well out of breath, yet knowing the urgency of reaching the car above them they hurried through it, coming out on the western side of the highway at the National Forest Service sign. Erasmus picked up the pace, "C'mon, we're almost there!"

Marie-Thérèse looked up to the car, seeing it still parked on the side of the highway. "It looks like we didn't get a ticket," she said.

"That's good!" Erasmus shouted back, the noise of the highway wind overpowering their voices.

They ran together to the place where they had first crossed the highway and waiting until the way was clear their feet picked up pace again, running, or again rather stumbling, across the double-yellow line back to their car. Erasmus was the first to reach the parked SUV on the far side of the highway. He looked back to see Marie-Thérèse leaping over the snow pile that had been such a trouble for her to cross earlier. Passed the last obstacle, she unlocked the car and opened the driver's door, climbing back into her seat and quickly turning the ignition to start the heater going. They both shivered, their bodies far colder than either of them had remembered being in years past. Yet their hearts were beating warmth, the love between them keeping them cosy and happy together.

Marie-Thérèse put the car into reverse, allowing herself enough room to ensure their romance wasn't a quick one, before turning the car to the left, and merging back into the southbound lanes on State Highway 16. They sped away from the trailhead, tunnel, stairway, and waterfall below. Far beneath them, the cardinals continued to sing, flying wing in wing along with the soft breeze below the level of the highway.

"Okay, so where is the turn off, Erasmus?" Marie-Thérèse asked, a sparkle still in her eye.

"It'll be a covered bridge. On our left," he replied, taking hold of the map once again. "Don't worry, I won't get distracted by some white tail this time."

"Excuse me?" Marie-Thérèse shot back.

"White tailed deer, there was a deer."

"Sure there was."

"O deer..."

Marie-Thérèse smiled, "I love your puns."

"I can be quite punny, honey."

Marie-Thérèse laughed, "Whatever you say, *mon chérie.* »

They drove on through the woods again, now leaving the wider four lane highway for a far narrower, more local two-lane thoroughfare. "It shouldn't be too much further," Erasmus said, following their location on his map. "That said, we do have a slight problem..."

"What's that?"

"It's getting dark, and I'm starting to have trouble seeing the map."

Marie-Thérèse paused for a moment to think, "Well, you said we're looking for a covered bridge?"

"Yeah."

"Alright, so let's look for a covered bridge. It's bound to be illuminated."

"Do you think so?"

"Yeah, how else are drivers at night going to avoid hitting the bridge when they should go over it?"

"Fair point," Erasmus muttered.

He was amazed at how little their regular conversation had changed since that kiss. Then again, he was still a fair bit uncertain about what to do about it. *"Maybe she is too,"* he thought. *"Then again, this isn't the time to ask. She's driving."*

They crossed the Ellis River on a regular old road bridge and soon saw ahead of them the covered bridge they'd been looking for. « C'est là ! » Erasmus pointed.

« Ô, excellent ! » Marie-Thérèse set her sights on safely manoeuvring the car so it would go through the bridge and not hit it.

They pulled up in front of it and saw a yield sign, warning them to wait for oncoming vehicles. Seeing none ahead of them, Marie-Thérèse slowly pulled up and onto the bridge, feeling the surface below their wheels change from concrete to wood in a most surreal of moments in the twenty-first century. Gingerly they crossed the covered bridge, feeling each plank beneath them creak with the arrival of yet another car.

"It looks like there's a pedestrian side to this bridge too," Erasmus said, noticing the footpath alongside them in the pale twilight.

"Good, let's come back here in the morning."

"Deal!"

"So, where do we go now?"

"It looks like we follow Main Street up to the school and then keep straight. The inn'll be up the hill," Erasmus replied, running his finger along the map.

"Great, so we're close then."

"We're in the village now."

"Will any of the villagers be out to greet us?"

"I don't know, but there seems to be a Native American statue over there in front of that tavern," Erasmus noted, "and look, there's the local constable too!"

"It's almost like we're back in New York."

"I know, there's a village full of people here."

They continued up Main Street, staying straight at the school and passing by the Post Office and a couple of other shops before ascending uphill again.

"There, it's on the right," Marie-Thérèse pointed, seeing the inn's sign along the roadside.

Erasmus watched as she left the road and pulled into the lane in front of the inn. "It looks so New England!" he said, seeing the white building with its broad porch.

"Yes, and we're just in time to get our names in for dinner," Marie-Thérèse replied, thinking of how long it had been since they last ate on the train while speeding through eastern Connecticut and western Rhode Island.

Marie-Thérèse found a parking spot close to the front door of the inn and let the SUV take a rest from its journeying. She too yearned for the warmth of their room and a nice meal. Opening the car door, the cool breeze, now without even more warmth owing to the disappearance of the Sun below the mountains for the long winter's night made her yearn even more for the warmth of a nice room. Marie-Thérèse stepped down out of the car, Erasmus quick to follow her lead. He walked to the back of the vehicle, looking at the trunk in front of him.

"Let's leave our things in the trunk for now, okay. I don't think we'll need them when we check in," Erasmus advised.

"Good thinking."

They stepped out behind the car and walked along the lane to the front steps of the inn, where with a less ginger sense of adventure than at the waterfall they climbed up the steps onto the deck above. From there, all that was needed was a quick turn of the old cold brass door handle for the inn's front door to swing open and its old wooded interior to reveal itself to them.

It was a very old house, one that dated back to colonial times. The wooden interiors reminded Erasmus of the taverns he'd seen on Long Island and in the Hudson Valley that had been visited by Washington, Hamilton, and other notable revolutionaries during and just after that war. In front of the door were the stairs leading to the upper floor of the inn, while to the left was the old parlour, perhaps the oldest room in the building when it was just another farmhouse nestled in the north woods of New Hampshire. Within the fireplace he could hear embers crackling and he yearned for their warmth. Yet his attention was instantly drawn by a dry alto voice coming from the other side of the hall.

"What brings you to my inn?"

Erasmus turned around and laid eyes on an older woman, her white hair and furrowed brow well suited to the inn in which she lived and worked. She wore a purple charvet dress, whose large pluming shoulders stood in sharp contrast to her narrow-corseted waist.

Marie-Thérèse turned to her, "Are you the inkeeper?"

"Yes. I am Honoria Inkpenne," replied the woman in purple.

"Ah, it's a pleasure to meet you Mrs. Inkpenne. We have a room reserved."

"Your name?" Mrs. Inkpenne asked, taking her pen from its stand on the reception desk and opening the reservation book.

"Merlinais."

"You are Canadian, I take it?" Mrs. Inkpenne inquired, running the pen down that day's page to see for the name in question.

"Yes."

"I'll need to see your passport," she commanded dryly. Mrs. Inkpenne looked up to Erasmus, "Are you Canadian too?"

"No, ma'am. I'm from Missouri."

"A Midwesterner. Few of your kind ever venture into my inn."

"It's quite the distance to travel," he chuckled.

"Yes, it is. But you do not sound like you live in the Midwest any longer."

"No, I live in New York."

"Ah and are you in the theatre?" she asked, her accent bizarrely antiquated.

"Em, no. I'm a computer coder."

"Ah shame."

Marie-Thérèse handed her passport over, the Canadian coat of arms shimmering in the low light of the inn. « Merci, mademoiselle, » Mrs. Inkpenne said, peeling the passport from Marie-Thérèse's grasp.

Marie-Thérèse was curious about the inkeeper and her dress. "Have you lived here a long time, Mrs. Inkpenne?" she asked gently.

"O yes, for many years," Mrs. Inkpenne replied, looking up at Marie-Thérèse from the reservation book, peering out at her from over her thin wired spectacles.

"How very nice."

"Yes, it is a pleasant place to be," Mrs. Inkpenne replied, writing something two thirds of the way down the page. "Here you are, Miss Merlinais. I see you have booked a room for two. Is this gentleman staying with you?"

"Yes, he is."

"I need to see some identification, sir. What's your name?"

Erasmus stepped up to the desk, pulling his driver's license out of his wallet, which rested in its usual spot in his coat. "Plumwood, Erasmus Plumwood, ma'am."

"Plumwood, you say? That's an unusual name. Is your family English?"

"Yes, though my father's family came to America a long time ago. They settled in Philadelphia I believe."

Mrs. Inkpenne looked up at Erasmus, "Your face looks familiar, have I seen you somewhere before?"

Erasmus was slightly unnerved by this, "I dunno, maybe."

"In any case, are you two related in any way?" Mrs. Inkpenne asked, seemingly testing their qualifications for sharing a room.

"Well, he's my boyfriend," Marie-Thérèse said, smiling and gently folding her hand around Erasmus's left arm.

"Ah. Very well then, here is your passport, Miss Merlinais, and your identification card, Mr. Plumwood. You will be staying in Room 8. It's just upstairs. Please remember to keep the noise down after ten o'clock."

"We'll bear that in mind," Erasmus confirmed, nodding his head.

"Can we make reservations for dinner now?" Marie-Thérèse asked.

"O yes, if you wish. When would you like to come down for dinner?" Mrs. Inkpenne asked.

"O, is there an opening at six o'clock?" Marie-Thérèse asked.

"That's rather early," Mrs. Inkpenne contended.

"Yes, I'm sorry, Mrs. Inkpenne, but we've been travelling all day and haven't eaten since eleven."

"Ah I see, well it looks like we have a table for two available at six," Mrs. Inkpenne replied, looking at the dinner reservation book for the evening.

« Excellent, merci beaucoup ! » Marie-Thérèse said, smiling and lowering her head in a demi-bow.

Mrs. Inkpenne acknowledged the gesture, curtseying in response. Returning to her normal posture, she turned about and collected an old brass key in her long spindly fingers, the lace cuff of her narrow right sleeve accentuating the shape and length of her forearm well. "Here is your key, please ensure that you do not lose it."

Marie-Thérèse took it in hand, "Thank you. I'll be most careful with this."

"Good," Mrs. Inkpenne said, her face still neutral, smileless, yet not necessarily grimacing.

"We'll just go outside and collect our luggage."

"Very well, good evening to you both," the innkeeper said, nodding as Erasmus opened the front door and stepped outside.

Marie-Thérèse followed Erasmus out of the inn, closing the big wooden front door behind her. "There's something strange about that woman," Erasmus whispered, facing away from the windows.

Marie-Thérèse nodded, "Yes, most unusual." She turned to look back at the inn, catching the window next to the front door in the corner of her eye. She could swear that Mrs. Inkpenne had left her place behind the desk where she had just been not more than a breath before. « Non, ce n'est pas possible, » she thought.

Erasmus went out to the car and watched as Marie-Thérèse activated the back door from a distance, still descending the steps from the front porch. He took both their suitcases in hand, each in its own turn, and set them down on the snowy ground behind the car. Marie-Thérèse collected her own, and Erasmus his, and they returned on their way back to the steps, up the steps themselves, and through the front door back into the inn. Mrs. Inkpenne was in the parlour, stoking the fire. Her dress, as Marie-Thérèse had assumed, reached to just above the heels of her boots. It had to have been at least a century old, and while the fabric didn't seem worn down, the dress itself was certainly of a style and age that seemed out of place in the vicinity of Erasmus's and Marie-Thérèse's own attire.

Erasmus began making his way up the stair, taking the sharp right hand turn at the first landing and coming to the top of the staircase with some difficulty, his suitcase feeling heavier than it had when they left their apartment in New York that morning. At the top of the stair he quickly noticed the room numbers ascending to the right, eastwards, along the corridor. Walking in that direction he came to their room, No. 8. Marie-Thérèse wasn't far behind him, their room key in hand. She set down her suitcase and inserting the key into the door heard it unlock and the hinges softly creak open.

The room was nice, comfortable. It's twin beds cosy and warm compared to the frigid cold air outside. Marie-Thérèse led the way in, looking around at what was on offer. There was a TV up atop the dresser in the centre of the room, directly across from the joint nightstand, upon which rested a lamp that served its kind well lighting that entire portion of the room. The room itself was small, but not too terribly small, big enough certainly for two adults to be comfortable in their own space together, as Marie-Thérèse and Erasmus had intended when they booked it online on Friday evening. The bathroom was just beyond the beds, in a dormer, its permanently frosted window offering privacy for anyone using the tub or toilet.

"Which bed do you want?" Erasmus asked.

"I'm fine with the one by the window, if you're okay with that."

"Yeah, that'll be good," Erasmus said, setting his suitcase down on the luggage rack that had been folded leaning against the wall between the dresser and the door. Marie-Thérèse found a second luggage rack in the closet, which was located past Erasmus next to the door. Opening their respective suitcases, they began to unpack. Erasmus first took off his overcoat, letting his yellow sweater shine brightly in the dimly lit room. Marie-Thérèse removed her grey overcoat and blue woollen scarf, laying them down at the foot of the bed. Her blue turtleneck fitted her form perfectly, as all of her outfits generally did, certifying and reaffirming her abilities as a fashion-minded individual. Erasmus looked up at her and smiled. She caught his smile and returned it back to him, her cheeks reddening as she did.

They continued unpacking, emptying their suitcases to allow for their dirty laundry to have a place to live until they could make it back to New York in five days. Five days together here, away from everything, away from everyone. Five days to explore and learn what it meant to be Erasmus and Marie-Thérèse, not just the best friends, but the couple. *"We're a couple!"* Erasmus thought, excited at the idea. *"My girlfriend is standing right there in front of me!"*

Marie-Thérèse looked back at him, "Why do you think didn't we say anything to each other before?"

"I dunno," Erasmus pensively replied, "I guess I was afraid to ask."

Marie-Thérèse continued folding her clothes silently for a moment as Erasmus watched, unsure if he had just said a good thing or a bad thing. Finally, she made her mind up, "Me too," she said, looking at him, pushing her bangs back from her eyes.

"You too?"

"I was afraid to ask as well."

They stood there silently.

"Well, now we both know. We said the words to each other," Erasmus said, walking over to her.

"Yes."

"I love you, Marie-Thérèse Merlinais."

« Et je t'aime aussi, Erasmus Plumwood. »

They kissed again, a long kiss that pushed all other thoughts from their minds. They were there, together. All the world around them meant little in that moment. Marie-Thérèse and Erasmus had each other, and that alone was a wonderful thing.

5

The Noel Inn

Marie-Thérèse was a beautiful woman, one who would doubtlessly stand out in a crowded room. She had a gracefulness that seemed to elevate a room when she entered, especially when she was dressed in more formal evening attire. Deciding to celebrate their newly recognised congeniality, Marie-Thérèse and Erasmus decided to wear their nicest clothes to their first dinner as a couple, their first real date. Marie-Thérèse wondered if this sort of giddy fluttering that they felt would last, or if they were in a proper flitterwochen of their own accord at this moment. Erasmus had been kind enough to go into the bathroom to change, giving Marie-Thérèse the comfort of the bedroom. While he fumbled about, knocking his right elbow into the white porcelain sink at least once, Marie-Thérèse merely smiled at how clumsy her boyfriend was. A real klutz.

As she zipped up the back of her velvety dress, the pattern of mistletoe and red and yellow irises came together in a flat pattern across her shoulders. The fabric flared out well at her waist, giving an elegant shape to her form. She sat down on a chair, and let her stockinged feet slide gently into her heels, the heel proper extending around 9 cm in height, or what Marie-Thérèse called "average." She walked over to her suitcase, and pulled from a pocket a black box, which closed with a small bronze clasp. Flipping the clasp upward, she pulled back the box's lid to reveal a silver necklace with opals encased in its face, their gems glistening in the electric light that illuminated their bedroom. Marie-Thérèse turned to her makeup bag, which sat on the top of the dresser. Unzipping it, she took out a soft wintery-blue cat-eye eyeshadow and a red lipstick, applying both with an ease that comes with a lifetime of experience. Looking in the mirror at her reflection, Marie-Thérèse thought for a moment about her hair. It was still down, loose and flowing, as she'd left it when they left New York that morning. « C'est bien comme ça, »[10] she muttered to herself, looking over to the bathroom door.

Erasmus was nearing the end of his dressing, the suspenders raised over his shoulders, his shirt properly tucked in. He raised his collar to put on a silk blue and yellow necktie that he'd quickly grabbed out of his suitcase without much consideration for its colour coordination. He draped it over his collarbone, tying it about his neck in a methodical manner that betrayed the fact that, like many men, he only really knew one knot for tying neckties. Looping the necktie about itself

---

[10] "It's fine as is."

twice, he took the front end and fed it through the knot downwards, creating a far firmer knot. Finally pulling the necktie upwards, Erasmus remembered why he normally didn't wear neckties as he felt its strain upon his throat. With a sense of finality, perhaps influenced by the sudden decrease of oxygen in the upper reaches of his body, Erasmus placed the remaining back half of the necktie into the loop behind its face, holding the back into place, at least until a strong wind intersected it. Erasmus turned to the coat hook on the back of the door and taking a cashmere Robin Hood green sweater in hand he let that fall over his head and drape itself onto his shoulders, forming a cosy layer over his shirt. He looked down at his wrists and folded the sweater's cuffs back under themselves to reveal the white of his shirt cuffs beneath. Erasmus turned back to the coat hook and took his suitcoat in hand, the well woven fabric soft and gentle to the touch. He cautiously put it on, not wanting to tear the coat before dinner.

Erasmus looked at himself in the mirror still amazed at the reality of his new predicament. "We kissed, we kissed," he whispered, staring into the reflection of his eyes in the glass.

He heard Marie-Thérèse zip something closed outside the door, and presumed she must be waiting for him. Not wanting to stall her too much more, Erasmus turned away from his image and opened the door, walking out to a scene from a John Singer Sargent portrait. « Ma chérie, tu es radiante ! » he stumbled in a breathy cry.

« Merci, » she replied, the biggest smile she'd had on her face in years radiating a glowing warmth into the darkened room. Marie-Thérèse stood up from her chair, her heels giving her enough height to match Erasmus. "Shall we go?"

"Yes, I'm starving," Erasmus said, stepping forward to her.

As he came closer to her she stepped away from him, walking to their room's front door and turning the brass handle, opening the door wide. She held it for Erasmus, « Après tu. »[11]

Erasmus smiled wide and stepped through the doorway. He waited against the railing of the staircase for Marie-Thérèse to close the door and follow after him. As she locked the door he stepped forward, holding out his arm for her. She smiled at him, "It's too narrow here, Erasmus. Downstairs."

"Okay," Erasmus said, leading the way down the staircase, this time more observantly of his footsteps not wanting to tumble far and hard in his nice suit.

Marie-Thérèse followed after him, watching the front desk to see if Honoria Inkpenne was still there at the same post as she had been a little while before. With no woman in purple in sight, Marie-Thérèse

---

[11] "After you."

descended the stair to the waiting Erasmus, whose outstretched arm she took. They walked together arm-in-arm around the corner past the front desk and to the dining room, where the maître d' held court. He was a younger man, with sharp black hair slicked back with some sort of gel. His face was not quite as pale as Erasmus's or Marie-Thérèse's, but in the darkened mood lighting of the place he seemed to be so. He wore a brown tweed suit with a polka-dotted blue bowtie crowning the collar of his crisp white shirt. "Good evening, ma'am, sir," he said smiling, "Do you have a reservation?"

"Yes, it's for Merlinais for two," Marie-Thérèse replied, leaning closer into Erasmus.

"Very good, if you'd like to follow me please," the maître d' replied, taking a pair of menus in hand from beneath the podium and guiding the pair to their table.

The dining room was a vast open space, built at varying times for varying purposes since the colonial era. In the far corner near a doorway that led to the inn's little library sat a musician at an upright piano, playing Gershwin and Irving Berlin love songs softly for the congregated diners. They were seated in the back of the dining room, in the section where the floorboards creaked rather more loudly than near the front, the part that had been the original dining room of the old colonial farmhouse. Erasmus and Marie-Thérèse took seats across from each other. The maître d' leaned down and placed the menus in front of each of them, "Your server will be right with you," he said, bowing slightly.

"Thank you," Marie-Thérèse replied, smiling at him.

As the maître d' turned and walked back to his podium on the far side of the restaurant, Marie-Thérèse looked at Erasmus, a big smile on her face.

Erasmus smiled back, the silence echoing from their curved lips. "Well, here we are," he stammered.

"Yes."

"It's a nice place, a neat old New England country inn."

"It's very English for sure."

"Very," she said, taking the menu in hand. She was surprised to see a mix of American and German options printed on it.

Erasmus looked at his as well, scanning it for something that he would enjoy but that would make him seem well cultured for his elegant *chérie* from Montréal. He was unsure of what to say and figured that the menu would serve as a way to pass the time before their long silences continued.

"O look, the wine list," Marie-Thérèse said, finding a small booklet on the edge of their table leaning up against the windowsill. She opened it and peered in the limited light down at the vintages on offer below.

After a few moments, for it rarely took Marie-Thérèse Merlinais more than that to make up her mind about a good glass of wine, she offered the volume to Erasmus, for his own oenophilic election. Erasmus knew some wines, his grandfather loved Chianti and his father always appreciated a good Argentine Malbec, but Erasmus was never much of an oenophile. He looked down the list but found himself more confounded than reassured by what was on offer. There were some California wines, but most of the list was French and Austrian. Erasmus noticed her gaze falling upon him, he set down the booklet and gazed back, raising his eyebrows in quick succession. Marie-Thérèse caught the look with all its comic force and let out a loud laugh, embarrassing herself in the process.

Erasmus breathed deeply, the tension lifting from the table. He reached out and held her hand, rubbing his fingers against hers. Their hands were cold, even colder as they were sitting next to a window. Nevertheless, they were warm together, happy together. "I don't know what to say," he whispered across the table to her.

Marie-Thérèse smiled back, "Here's a secret for you. I don't know what to say either."

"Do you know what's always been my favourite animal?" Erasmus asked, reaching for something to talk about.

"You love river otters, right?"

"Yeah, they're cute. But I've always loved the moose. Such fantastic animals!" Erasmus proclaimed, leaning back in his chair.

"They're neat, for sure, but they're a bit dangerous too."

"True, but aren't all the best animals?"

"I suppose so," Erasmus affirmed, seeing their waiter arriving.

The waiter was an older man, his dark grey hair betraying his past brown locks. "Good evening, my name is Karl, I'll be serving you this evening. What would you like to drink?"

Marie-Thérèse looked up at him with assurance, "The Chinon, please."

"An excellent choice, madam. And sir?"

"Um...," Erasmus began, picking up the wine list again, "I'll have the same."

"Very good. Would you prefer to share a bottle?"

Marie-Thérèse and Erasmus looked at each other, contemplating the offer. Marie-Thérèse nodded, "Yes, I think we will."

"Very good. Thank you both," the waiter bowed his head slightly, backing away and turning about, quick-footing across the restaurant to the kitchen on the east side of the room.

The couple returned to their previous staring contest, an insecurity in what to say still the loudest thing at their table. "Well, the wine ought to be good," commented Erasmus, trying to ease the silence.

"Yes. I love Chinon," Marie-Thérèse replied, taking Erasmus's hands into hers.

"Where's Chinon again?"

"It's on the Loire in France."

"But I thought Loire wines were mostly whites?" Erasmus asked.

"They are, but Chinon is an exception. A red grape in a sea of white. It has such a rich taste."

"Ah, okay."

They paused as the pianist took a quick break from his playing to take a drink.

"Looks like he has a pint there," Marie-Thérèse noted.

"O yeah. I guess they have a bit of everything here."

"Well, the U.S. is known for being more of a beer culture than a wine one," Marie-Thérèse noted.

"True. My Dad much prefers beer to wine."

"Why's that do you think?" Marie-Thérèse asked.

"I'm not sure. I guess that's probably just what he grew up around."

"Is his family English originally?" Marie-Thérèse asked.

"Probably. They've been in America for a very long time. They were from one of the Mid-Atlantic colonies, New York or Pennsylvania, I think."

"So they might've been Dutch?"

"Yeah, it's possible. I don't know where our name comes from though."

"Plumwood is an unusual name," Marie-Thérèse noted as the waiter returned with their bottle of Chinon.

"Here you are," he said, popping up the cork and pouring it into their glasses, first pouring the drink into Marie-Thérèse's cup before filling Erasmus's.

"Thank you," Erasmus said, raising his glass to the waiter.

"You're very welcome, sir. Have you had time to look over the menu?"

Erasmus looked to Marie-Thérèse to speak first. "Yes, I think we have," she replied, taking her menu in hand and scanning her eyes across its long body again. "Could I have the flank steak?" she asked.

"How would you like that cooked?" the waiter replied, scribbling something mildly illegible on his notepad.

"Medium, please."

"Perfect, madam." The waiter turned to Erasmus, "and for you, sir?"

"Could I have the scallops, please?"

"Certainly, sir. I'll bring those out to you when they're ready." The waiter bowed his head and retired to the kitchen.

"Great service here," Erasmus noted.

"Yes, they seem to be quite observing," Marie-Thérèse replied, holding the stem of her glass with her finger tips. She raised it to Erasmus. "What should we drink to?"

Erasmus smiled a big corny smile, "To us."

"To us."

Marie-Thérèse and Erasmus clinked their glasses together, taking tender sips of their wine.

Erasmus looked down at the glass, "O this is good!"

Marie-Thérèse smiled, "It's one of my father's favourites, the one that got him into the business."

"Do you have a favourite wine?" Erasmus asked, lightly running the foot of his glass along the stem of hers.

Marie-Thérèse looked down at the sliding glasses before her, « Pourquoi qu'est qu'il fait ça ?»[12] she thought, answering, "O, I do really enjoy these Chinon, though a good Savoie is also a nice option. How'bout you?"

Erasmus thought for a moment. He enjoyed wine but always had trouble remembering their names. "I think it was a Tyrolean wine that I really liked, or maybe Austrian. It definitely had a German-sounding name."

"Blaufränkisch?" Marie-Thérèse inquired, taking another sip of her glass.

"Yeah, that was it!" he started, "It had a really nice taste to it."

"I've had one before, in Vienna. Such a good wine."

"What'd they pair it with?" Erasmus asked, taking a larger sip, nay a drink, from his glass.

"Goulash."

"Ooo, the Hungarian kind?"

"Indeed."

"I wonder if there's a good goulash place around here?" Erasmus asked, his glass now nearing 1/3rd empty.

"There might be," Marie-Thérèse quipped, "but I don't know how many Hungarians ended up here in New Hampshire."

Marie-Thérèse took another drink of her wine. "You know, Erasmus," she started, "I often wonder about you."

Erasmus sipped.

"Why'd you go into computer science in the first place?"

Erasmus thought for a moment. "Y'know, these sorts of questions remind me that I often don't really know why I do the things that I do."

---

[12] "Why is he doing that?"

Marie-Thérèse raised an eyebrow as Erasmus thought for a moment.

"I guess I just never liked people that much. Computers are easier to predict than people, they run on mathematics, on ones and zeroes. People are unreliable, unpredictable. They run on whims and fancies. I just like the regularity of computers."

"So, do I remind you of a computer then?" Marie-Thérèse retorted, getting at his goat.

"No, you're better than a computer, and far better than most humans. I love how sensible you are, how straight-forward and clear thinking you can be. Sure, you're analytical, but you're also warm, charming, and caring. And you're beautiful too."

Marie-Thérèse's cheeks glowed a bright red at that declaration.

Erasmus noticed, and though he felt tense he nevertheless saw it as his Rubicon moment. *"Alea jacta est,"*[13] he thought.

Marie-Thérèse leaned in close, Erasmus followed her lead, unsure what she was going to do. As he leaned in Marie-Thérèse lifted her chin slightly and kissed him on the cheek, whispering « *De toi c'était un bon compliment.* »

Erasmus turned his cheek to face her, kissing her on the lips with the tenderness of his love. She requited his kindness, attracting the attention of some of their fellow diners. The pianist who had been playing of all things *Waltzing Matilda* in the background switched to a lyrical arrangement of Stephen Foster's *Hard Times Come Again No More*. A middle-aged woman at the table next to them took particular glee at seeing the expressive young couple, "How long have you been together?" she asked as Marie-Thérèse and Erasmus leaned back in their chairs, taking sips of their wine.

Marie-Thérèse replied, her eyes glinting at Erasmus's, "O, just since this afternoon."

The woman was taken aback. "You met this afternoon?!"

Marie-Thérèse feigned realizing what confusion she'd caused, "Oooo, no, we've been sharing an apartment for a few years now, but we've only been officially a couple since this afternoon."

"O, I see!" the woman, on her second Manhattan, shouted, "Well congratulations on your engagement!"

Erasmus darted a shocked look at Marie-Thérèse. Marie-Thérèse too looked surprised at how this conversation had turned out. «*C'est vrai, je voudrais marier Erasmus, mais je ne veux pas ça maintenaient,* »[14] Marie-Thérèse thought.

---

[13] "The die is cast."

[14] "It's true, I'd like to marry Erasmus, but not quite now."

"What the hell happened? Are we engaged now?!" Erasmus's mind raced like a basset hound excited yet terrified at the sight of its first garden gnome.

"Um, ma'am, we're not engaged yet," Erasmus tried to explain, "We've just started officially dating."

Erasmus's protests were drowned out by the woman, her husband who was far drunker than her, his shot glass seeming to have sprung a leak, and a family of five sitting at a table nearby. The woman next to them told the pianist who began to play, more loudly, the wedding march from Mozart's *Le Nozze di Figaro* to which he sang:

"It's a happy day for a wedding,
Let the bells peel and ring
It's a joyous day for a marriage
A day when we can all sing!"

Marie-Thérèse realised how far her joke had gone and looked on as the rest of the diners joined in on the song. Her face became red with embarrassment, while Erasmus seemed to melt down in his chair, avoiding the throng of misinformed well-wishers who surrounded their table. Their smiles were like bared tigers' teeth.

Erasmus noticed Mrs. Inkpenne standing in the kitchen doorway, watching the sudden burst of merriment in her establishment. She seemed above it all, foreign to the jovial fray happening before her, distant as if in another world. Yet her eyes were sharply focused on Erasmus's, as if she were trying to communicate something to him. *"She knows, she knows it's not true,"* he thought, hoping that all this uproar would just go away and they could enjoy their dinner together.

Marie-Thérèse caught Erasmus's gaze and turned to see Mrs. Inkpenne staring back at him, « *Qu'est qu'ils pensent ?* »[15] she thought.

As the pianist changed his tune, playing instead the *Sailor's Hornpipe*, the revellers began to dance together, rising from their tables and forming a large circle around the dining room. Erasmus watched as they bumped into tables and chairs, kicking their feet back and forth to the rhythm of the music. As each dancer passed their table their head turned, revealing a startling face; some snarling, some gleeful, some smiling, some angry. "What's wrong with these people?" he asked Marie-Thérèse, shouting over the hubbub.

"I don't know!" she cried. Marie-Thérèse rose from their table, and saw their waiter attempting to bring their food over from the kitchen, but the dancers were blocking his way. She was overwhelmed and annoyed at how gullible all these people were. "Stop it! Stop it!" she shouted, but to no avail.

---

[15] "What are they thinking?"

"But we're not engaged!" Erasmus thought terrified at this increasingly unruly sight.

A voice came from across the room. Erasmus looked up and caught the eagle eyes of Mrs. Inkpenne from the kitchen, whose face was covered every other beat by the passing dancers. She stared directly at him, her eyes sharper than any other he'd ever seen. Her lips weren't moving, yet he could distinctly hear that monotone voice. *"I know!"*

Erasmus lurched upright in bed, his face covered in sweat despite the freezing air from outside. He felt warmer than usual, which again didn't make sense. Regaining his senses, he looked down and saw Marie-Thérèse curled up beside him, her arms around his shoulders. He hadn't remembered falling asleep with her and was very sure they hadn't done anything else. Yet there she was, in his bed, lying there next to him. In her sleep she was muttering something in French. She breathed deeply and rolled more onto her back. The bed wasn't quite wide enough for both of them, but it was still comfortable.

Erasmus laid back down onto his right side and thought for a moment, his eyes facing the front door. He could still see the bodies of the dancers flying before him, the skirts of the women flaring with each movement of their feet in a counter-clockwise motion. The music was still intoxicating, or perhaps it was the wine. "How much did I drink?" he muttered, closing his eyes.

Morning came with the Sun's calling, its rays creeping through the room's window that overlooked the dormer that enclosed the bathroom. As its rays steadily extended further and further into the room, they at last fell upon Marie-Thérèse's face. Her eyes began to flutter, the sudden flash of light upon their lids startling their deep sleep. She attempted to raise up her right arm to cover her eyes, but found it pinned down by a pillow next to her. She turned her head to see and was shocked to find Erasmus's head on the pillow next to her. *«Qu'est qui se passe ?»* she muttered.

Erasmus was awoken by her voice, the latter hours of his sleep far shallower than before. He rolled over to face her, finding her with a bemused look on her face. *« Bon matin, ma chérie. »*

« Bon matin, » she replied uncertainly.

Erasmus noticed the caution in her voice. "How do you feel?"

"Hungover," she replied, removing her right arm from beneath his pillow. "Just tell me one thing, did we–"

"I don't think so," he affirmed. "Can you remember last night?" he asked.

She sighed a bit, her brows furrowing, "I don't think so. How much did we drink do you think?"

"At least a bottle."

Marie-Thérèse sat up, she looked at Erasmus, "I don't know about you, but I had the strangest dreams."

"Me too! There were dancers and people congratulating us, and then there was Mrs. Inkpenne–"

"She was in your dream too?"

"Yeah," Erasmus replied, stopping and thinking a moment about it. "It was like she was talking to me. Like she knew something about us that no one else knew."

"What'd everyone else in your dream know?" Marie-Thérèse asked, walking over to the mirror and rubbing her fingers through her hair.

"They thought we were engaged."

She stopped and stared at him in the mirror. "Engaged?"

"Yeah."

"We didn't get engaged last night, did we?" she asked, her face going pale.

"I don't think so, at least it didn't seem like it to me. I can tell you that I don't have a ring."

"That's probably for the better, y'know. We're not really at that stage in our relationship yet," she said, going into the bathroom, taking her toothbrush and toothpaste in hand.

"Yeah, we're *knot* there yet," he said, a sly grin on his face.

Marie-Thérèse rolled her eyes as she began to brush her teeth. "What time is it?" she asked.

Erasmus looked at the alarm clock on the nightstand between their beds, "It's 7:20."

"O good, then we haven't missed breakfast," she called back, her electric toothbrush rather loud in the tiled bathroom.

Erasmus's stomach felt a tad upset, but not too terribly that he couldn't eat a pancake or two.

Marie-Thérèse finished brushing her teeth, spit out the remaining toothpaste, and leaned her head out the open doorway again. "I'm going to shower first, okay."

"Fine by me," came the reply. Erasmus leaned back in bed. He opened the drawer of the nightstand next to him to see if there'd be any books in there worth reading. There was the usual staple, a standard Protestant Bible, and an overly large book about an American graduate student travelling in Europe.[16] He picked the second book, the big one, and picked a random spot near the middle to read. He read about this student's adventures in Finland, *"such a neat country, I've always wanted to visit it."* as he heard the shower turn on and Marie-Thérèse step into the tub. The names of the Finnish cities, Helsinki, Turku, and the like seemed so foreign to Erasmus. Sure, his mother had read the old

---

[16] Coincidentally this book is available on Amazon. Look for the author of the volume you're reading and the word "Europe" together.

Assyrian, Babylonian, and Sumerian epics to him, and as a result Turku sounded an awful lot like Enkidu, Gilgamesh's best friend, *"but surely the names aren't related,"* he thought.

He thought about Gilgamesh and Enkidu, two dear friends from a far older time. Those stories always fascinated him as a child, perhaps because his mother could really animate them. She'd read them in her youth as well, wandering the halls of the British Museum after school to see the great winged lions that'd been brought to Bloomsbury from Nimrud in Iraq. She would stand in the long yet narrow halls that were lined with the great lion hunt scenes and read her tattered paperback English translation of Gilgamesh, a practice continued in her adulthood, only this time with a Babylonian version, cuneiform figures printed onto the page with all the benefits of the technology of the 1980s.

She once told Erasmus as a small boy, "If you stand here before the wounded lion who's standing strong and read aloud Gilgamesh and Enkidu's great hunt from the epic in Babylonian you can just hear that lion let out a roar!"

Erasmus remembered staring at the lion as his mother read the verse and was amazed to hear a distant roar sound from the lion's throat. The magic of that moment lived on with him, the lion's roar clamouring down through the ages. In his mind the image of Gilgamesh meeting the scorpion men, learning that he will never be able to restore Enkidu to life. The pain that brought the demigod down to mortality seemed to be unbearable but still it brought Gilgamesh into new life. Erasmus thought about that image, the wailing demigod at the feet of the scorpion men, as he stood and walked over to the window.

He looked out the window over the roof of the inn. Before him stood the woods, a good ten metres or so back from the inn itself, along the road that lead past the inn back towards the village green. Outside the snow was falling again, a softer early morning snow. It looked like it had been snowing for a few hours at least, as the grass before the trees was well covered, the snow piles rising up the trunks by a few centimetres as far as the northern winds would take them. The trees were bare of their leaves, the bark worn and grey in the winter winds whose cold breath had enveloped the leaves, causing them to shrivel and fall from the branches onto the forest floor below. What remained of those leaves surely had since decayed beneath the waves of snow that had fallen atop them in the intervening weeks. "Gilgamesh wouldn't have known about snow," Erasmus muttered to himself, fogging up the window with his breath.

Marie-Thérèse appeared from the bathroom, a towel about her person fastened beneath her shoulders, a second towel wrapped about her head like a turban shaped in the form of a kebab spit, letting the water soak out of her hair as she went about dressing herself. She walked over to the dresser, pulled open the top drawer where her things had been placed the evening before. Erasmus stood there and looked on, not sure quite what to do. Marie-Thérèse quickly caught on, turning to face him, "Just because we slept together last night doesn't mean you can watch me dress this morning. We're dating, we're not wedded yet. Get in the shower!"

Erasmus hurriedly collected his folded underclothes form their home in the second drawer in their room's dresser and left her be for his own showering. Marie-Thérèse smiled, thinking about how nervous he seemed to be at the very sight of her. That visit to the waterfall the day prior had changed Erasmus; he seemed to be far more conscious of her presence, far more so than he had ever been before. Sure, he'd recognised her when she was around, after all they decided to move in together because of their long conversations. *"You're here most of the time anyway, you'd might as well move in,"* Marie-Thérèse remembered saying to him late one April evening three years prior.

"Here?" he had asked, *"Isn't it a bit small for two people?"*

Erasmus made a good point there, after all Marie-Thérèse's dorm room was miniscule at most, nigh to a monastic cell at least. *"Well, if we're going to be living together then we ought to pool our money and find somewhere a little bit nicer,"* she'd replied, taking a sip of her red tea, bought from a Chinese grocer on 113th Street near Columbia.

Marie-Thérèse could remember the taste of that tea, it was a particularly strong one that her friend Liǔ Mǐn[17] had recommended. It wasn't to Marie-Thérèse's tastes though, and so she spent a good six months politely declining her friend's offers to refill Marie-Thérèse's tea chest with it. *« Le thé était une bonne idée pour ce p'tit déjeuner, »*[18] she muttered to herself. *« C'est possible qu'ils y auraient du thé blanc. »*[19]

Marie-Thérèse turned to her dresser and quickly donned her underclothes before choosing a white blouse, a slightly sharp looking forest green tunic that was thick enough as to act as a sweater, and a pair of black leggings. She dressed quickly as she could hear Erasmus was finished in the shower and was shaving. He wouldn't take too much longer. Pulling her tunic over her head, Marie-Thérèse collected a pair of socks from her dresser drawer and pulled them over her feet. She turned next to her suitcase where she'd kept a spare pair of boots that would go better with this outfit. Their black leather still had much of its shine from when she first bought them on Fifth Avenue that October.

---

[17] 栁敏

[18] "Tea is a good idea for [today's] breakfast."

[19] "It's possible that they'll have white tea."

As she zipped up the boots alongside her legs she heard the bathroom door handle turn.

Erasmus emerged from the bathroom in his undershirt, underpants and long underwear. A towel was loosely placed atop his head, as if attempting to wear it like Marie-Thérèse had only a few minutes prior. Marie-Thérèse looked at her friend with the bafflement of a mountain goat upon seeing a sheep with its head stuck in a fence and burst laughing. Erasmus smiled broadly, removing his right hand from behind his back to reveal his toothbrush. He held it aloft and struck a pose, sticking his hips out far to the left, letting his legs seem longer, like an elegant catwalk model. He made a face like a constipated poodle and burst into song full fortissimo,

"I've gotta feelin' do-do-do
That you're confused do-do-do
But here I am do-do-do
Standing here with yoooouuu!"

Erasmus began to dance a bizarre high-kneed clop, his arms flailing out and about without any real sense of purpose or reason. Marie-Thérèse sat down on the bed and laughed, beating the 3/4 rhythm on her thighs, her pale white hands dancing on pace with Erasmus's feet. Erasmus imagined a thrilling blues guitar riff as he danced and Marie-Thérèse sang her verse through bursts of laughter,

«Mon cher il y a tu-tu-tu
beaucoup des chansons tu-tu-tu
qui tu peux chanter tu-tu-tu
mais je chante ça avec tuuuuuu! »[20]

Erasmus laughed heartily, the silliness of their song becoming unbearable any longer. He bent over and held his stomach, laughing all the time. His towel had long since fallen from his head, leaving his dishevelled hair exposed. He looked up and felt his hair standing on edge, the vast majority of it rising up to greet the ceiling, which while still over a good metre above his head nevertheless seemed to have a gravitational attractiveness to the dark brunette locks that crowned his head. Erasmus gazed into the mirror at his reflection, "Excuse me for a minute, I need a comb."

He darted back into the bathroom and quickly combed his hair, creating his normally omnipresent part on the left temple while at the same time ensuring that his handiwork didn't turn into a combover. Erasmus was just as fast in returning to the bedroom as he had been in

[20] "My dear is there, you-you-you
many songs you-you-you
that you can sing you-you-you
but I sing that with youuuuuu!"

retreating to the safety of his comb. He'd seen enough of his reflection in the bathroom mirror and wasn't in the mood for anymore reflectiveness. Instead, he felt the cold air curving around his body, hugging him in its frigid boreal embrace. Erasmus went to the closet and chose a light blue button-down shirt, which he donned before picking his standard pair of black trousers and lowering his legs into them the right one before the left. Now trousered, he redonned the same yellow sweater that he'd worn the day before. It wasn't too gaudy, but it nevertheless reminded him of bananas. All the while Marie-Thérèse watched on from the foot of her bed. "You're like a lemur trying to get back up in the trees," she commented jokingly.

"I like lemurs. Amazing animals."

"Yeah," she replied. Marie-Thérèse remembered their visit to the lemur enclosure at the Kansas City Zoo two summers before, when she went west to visit the elder Plumwoods at their beautiful early-twentieth century home.

Erasmus turned to the dresser, withdrawing one of the more essential daily articles from within and belted his trousers into place. He pulled the belt tighter than sometimes before, a feat which always surprised him, but it made sense. Since he'd been working on his thesis, Erasmus hadn't eaten as much, and was frequently missing lunch on an almost daily basis. As a result, he'd lost a good 5 kilograms since the Fourth of July. That was actually the last time he had eaten a large lunch at the family barbeque back in Kansas City. Marie-Thérèse had never been much of a celebrator of the Fourth and was always back home in Montréal that week for Canada Day on the first anyway, so Erasmus normally took that week as a good time to go back to the heat of the Kansas City summer and spend Independence Day with his family.

Marie-Thérèse too noticed how tight Erasmus had pulled his belt. She'd been worried about his forgetfulness at lunchtime, concerned that this could end up being bad for his health. Sure, there'd been days where he had gone without food for ten or even twelve hours, but those especially grouchy days were few and further in between. Erasmus was always a bit of a light-hearted curmudgeon, someone who was fun to be around but could get annoyed easily. She especially knew that he didn't like boredom. That had never suited Erasmus Plumwood. As Erasmus filled his pockets, with his wallet, his phone, his driver's licence, Marie-Thérèse looked back at him, "What do you want to do today?" she asked.

He looked down at the top of the dresser, returning an inkpen to his right trouser pocket. "I don't know. How about breakfast for starters?"

"Sounds good to me."

As they descended the stairs, this time in less formal attire, Erasmus found the dining room much as he had dreamt it to be. Mrs. Inkpenne was there, seating her guests at the varied tables that stood seventeen-fold across the room. She sat the pair at a table near the one where they'd dined the evening prior. With an empty stomach and a longing for pancakes, Erasmus ordered to his heart's desire and breakfasted with all the joy of a child eating his favourite food. Marie-Thérèse in contrast ordered a plate of eggs, sausage links, and three pieces of toast which she buttered and covered with strawberry jam. Much to her delight, the inn had a small stock of white tea, which they served happily to the Montréalaise. It was a good start to what ought to be a good day. "A good day indeed," said Marie-Thérèse, sipping her tea.

Erasmus looked up from his apple juice, "I hope so."

Marie-Thérèse looked at him, a sense of wonder in her eyes. She was always more cognisant of the wider world than he. At this moment all he noticed was Marie-Thérèse sitting in front of him, and his large glass of apple juice that was now nearing half-full. She kept her eye on all around them, on their drinks, their table, their fellow diners, on Erasmus himself, on Mrs. Inkpenne who scanned the dining room from the maître d's podium, and on those unrealised in her reality but nevertheless observing on. She smiled and observed them over her cup of white tea.

6

Sleigh Ride

The snows did not melt with the rising of the Sun. Its warm rays tickled the white canvas that was stretched bare across the mountainsides and valleys in between, yet it had little effect on the fallen flakes already settled and gathered neatly in drifts on the soil. The northern winds continued to flourish, their resounding choruses as indefatigable as the melody that first created reality itself all those aeons ago. The snow, it seemed, was indominable, an incurable fact of life for the New Englanders who lived within its cold embrace for nigh half the year in their small, northern states. These old Yankees, the descendants of the fierce minutemen and Green Mountain Boys who had been resilient against the British advances at Bunker Hill and had pulled the guns of Fort Ticonderoga across the lakes and mountains to take their posts on the hills surrounding Boston were still today, just over thirteen generations later, as resilient as their ancestors had ever been.

Perhaps it was the weather, the extreme cold, the snow that defined half their lives. Perhaps it was their old Puritan brand of Christianity, now one faith of many practiced in New England, well and truly in the last century and a half alongside growing numbers of Catholics, Jews, Muslims, and so many more in between. New England, the cradle of the American North, the home of American abolitionism. New England, home to so many disparate peoples, yet even more snow. Let's face it, if you're looking for warm sunshine in December, New England isn't the place for you.[21]

Erasmus considered this reality as he stared out at the snow-covered driveway from the relative safety of the covered porch at the Noel Inn. Out in the snow stood Marie-Thérèse, bent over her hands thick in a snow pile. Though her back was turned to him, Erasmus nevertheless knew what must be coming next, the only good reason that anyone, even someone so used to the cold like Marie-Thérèse, would willingly stick their gloved hands into a large snow pile. He flinched as she swung about, flinging a freezing cold, yet perfectly spherical snowball at his head.

Erasmus misjudged his flinch enough that he managed to sway into the path of the oncoming sphere. It struck him square in the nose, the force of the blow causing it to turn a bright beet shade of red. Erasmus bent his neck, turning his face into his elbow instinctively. He quickly shook his head like a dog trying to dry itself and turned back to

---

[21] This is not a message from the Florida Tourism Board, they've got their own problems.

face Marie-Thérèse, picking up speed and leaping from the porch down onto the concrete drive below. His feet made contact as Erasmus envisioned their bathtub back in New York. He quickly felt the soles of his boots glide along the surface of the ice. He held his arms up behind his head and softened the blow to his skull and hair, before sliding forwards at a greater speed than Erasmus would have liked past the onlooking Montréalaise and feet-first square into the snow pile from which the weaponry of the morning had derived.

"Are you okay?!" Marie-Thérèse called, walking over to Erasmus's crumpled body which lay on the frozen ground, feet still imbedded in the snow.

Erasmus groaned, "Why the hell did I do that?"

Marie-Thérèse leaned over to help Erasmus prop himself up, "That was quite the slide."

"Yeah? Skeleton quality?"

"Almost, though your clothes aren't skin tight enough."

"Fair point," Erasmus muttered, pushing himself up to his feet. Erasmus turned about to see if any of the other guests at the inn had seen his fall. Hardly anyone was in sight, most still breakfasting in the dining room. Nevertheless Erasmus, could just make out a pale face in one of the windows of the inn's parlour, the pale pallor of Mrs. Inkpenne gazing back out at them. Her radiant blue eyes pierced what little warmth Erasmus felt in his body, leaving only cold, harsh, piercing cold within.

Erasmus turned away from the inn, and looked at Marie-Thérèse, "I'm a fool, aren't I."

"Only as much as you want to be," she replied, hugging him.

Erasmus felt the warmth of Marie-Thérèse's body and hugged her back. « Merci beaucoup ma chérie, » he whispered into her ear.

She kissed him on the cheek, her lip balm leaving a visible mark. "C'mon, let's go explore the grounds," she said, releasing him from her arms and taking his gloved hand in hers.

They walked away from the snow pile and back towards the inn, turning before the porch and walking towards some of the other buildings. There was an old house next to the inn that seemed to have been converted into more guest rooms, its red walls standing out in contrast to the white walls of the inn. It looked occupied, the curtains in some of the rooms fluttering from children playing, while other rooms remained darkened, their occupants still fast asleep despite the rising of Phaëton's chariot earlier that morning.

Past the house was a large barn. Marie-Thérèse looked at it for a moment, its great front beam stronger and taller than many others she had seen. "Do you want to go inside?"

"Sure," Erasmus replied, feeling the pain in his calves from his admittedly graceful slide into the snow.

They approached the barn and found a man in a heavy overcoat, thick trousers, and knee-high riding boots standing inside, feeding one of the horses. "Good morning," Marie-Thérèse said, approaching him.

The stable hand turned, surprised to hear anyone speaking to him. "Good mornin', are you from the inn?"

"Yes, we were just walking by and wanted to come in and see the horses."

"O, great," he replied, holding a feed bucket up towards the top of the gate of the third stall back on the right, setting its arms over the top of the gate and letting the stall's equine occupant enjoy a hearty breakfast. "M'name's Bill Doty, and these are the inn's team of horses."

"How many do you have?" Marie-Thérèse asked, looking around the barn.

"We have four here right now, enough to pull two sleighs if we need to."

Erasmus's ears perked up, "Did you say sleighs?"

"Yeah, we do sleigh rides for the guests, though occasionally they're needed if one of the trucks is out of gas."

"O wow!" Erasmus sighed. He'd wanted to go on a sleigh ride for years, though there was never quite the opportunity in either Kansas City or New York, and certainly not when he was visiting his family in London. *"It's like what the old song says"* he thought, Christmas carols ringing between his ears.

Marie-Thérèse stood near the front of the barn with Bill talking about horses as Erasmus began to internally ask himself perhaps the most important question of the month of December, *"Did I send my Mom her Christmas present?"*

He thought back through the preceding fortnight, scared that he might have made a crucial error. *"I don't think I've sent anything out to Kansas City..."* he thought, scared witless. Marie-Thérèse noticed the colour drain out of his face.

« *Qu'est qui c'est passe ?*» she asked, stepping towards him and placing a hand on his shoulder.

"Do you remember if I sent a Christmas present to my Mom?"

Marie-Thérèse looked back into his eyes, "You don't remember?"

"No?" Erasmus responded now unsure at what he'd sent her. "I didn't buy her a pair of socks, did I?"

"No, you bought her a book."

"A book?"

"Yeah, o c'mon, Erasmus, don't you remember? It was that big 700-page book with the woman on the front cover."

"The travel book?"

"Yes, that's the one."

"O good. She'll enjoy that."

Marie-Thérèse turned back to Bill, continuing to arrange their sleigh ride.

"Hey, M.T.?"

She turned to face Erasmus again, « Oui ?»

"What'd you get your Mom for Christmas?" he grinned.

"Olive oil and a granddaughter."

"A granddaughter, what?!"

Marie-Thérèse laughed, "I'm joking!"

Erasmus breathed a deep sigh of relief. He couldn't remember the night before, they drank too much wine for that. But he was pretty sure they quickly left their conscious reality for the sea of dreams in short order after retiring to their room after dinner. Apparently, Marie-Thérèse was far more certain of that.

"So, when should we be back?" Marie-Thérèse asked Bill having come to an agreed price for the sleigh ride.

"Come back at noon. I'll take the two of you on some of the unpaved roads through the woods here.

"That'll be lovely," Marie-Thérèse replied, smiling to him, "We'll be back just a little before noon."

"Good, thanks!" Bill replied, retiring into the barn to prepare the horses for the journey.

Marie-Thérèse walked back over towards Erasmus, still grinning like a cat that's just tricked another cat into biting its own tail. "Let's go see the spa."

"That sounds nice. Do they take walk-ins?"

"I doubt it. It's kind of a Christmas resort place, they're probably very busy this time of year.

"Yeah, true," Erasmus replied, following Marie-Thérèse's footsteps in the fallen snow.

They walked a little bit further up the hill, past ancient pines that had dwelt in the White Mountains for millennia, long before the arrival of the English and French colonists to this region of the Americas twenty generations before in the seventeenth century. Nevertheless, so much time had passed since the days before the mass logging that had dominated the great northern forests of New England and Québec since the colonial days. Twenty generations since the *Mayflower* caught sight of Cape Cod, for Marie-Thérèse's fellow Québécois it had been twenty-one generations since the first French colonists arrived along the shores of the Gulf of St. Lawrence. So much time had passed that it left the landscape and its people forever changed. Few traces of the indigenous peoples that once dwelt here in the White Mountains were left, the odd place name, the occasional family with indigenous ancestors. These mountains had become home to colonists and immigrants alike: English, French, Irish, German, Polish, and

Russian amongst others. The globe was certainly shrinking, with each passing generation as the many worlds upon its surface collided and combined.

The Spa was in an old carriage house, further up the hill near a large old country house, designed like a Swiss chalet. It had been greatly renovated since it was home to those elegant carriages and cabs that had carried whichever rich Boston brahmin or New York knickerbocker who used to own this land. Erasmus had a feeling that the inn and the carriage house hadn't always been under the same ownership, though he couldn't be sure in that assessment. "Who do you think used to live here?" Erasmus asked, gazing up at the high timber beams of the carriage house.

"Someone well-to-do for sure," Marie-Thérèse responded, looking up at it as well. The woodwork was enviable to be sure. The building's architecture reminded her of the lodges and ranger stations in the American national forests and parks. "This must be about a century old," she muttered, walking up to the façade of the building and placing her gloved palm onto one of the timber posts that held the roof aloft.

"I wonder, do you know, whenever I see buildings like this, I always seem to think of Teddy Roosevelt," Erasmus mused, turning to look at Marie-Thérèse.

"Why?"

"Well, he was the great environmentalist. Didn't he found the National Parks Service?"

"I don't know, you're the American."

"Touché," Erasmus jested.

Erasmus thought about the first President Roosevelt. His statue stood tall over the front steps of the Natural History Museum on Central Park West, not far from their apartment. Erasmus and Marie-Thérèse passed it often when they'd go for walks in Central Park. He always admired President Roosevelt's stamina and charisma, the stories, now many of them legends, about his momentous presidency, when the United States truly entered the twentieth century, had loomed large over Erasmus since he was a small child. "What colour do you think T.R.'s eyes were?" Erasmus pondered aloud.

Marie-Thérèse largely ignored the question. "Not sure," she muttered. Marie-Thérèse's attention was less on Theodore Roosevelt's eyes, long since dead yet still as vigorous in the American imagination as ever, and more on the current occupants of the carriage house.

She walked up to the big oaken doors, whose wooden frames held two twin large glass panes in place. The snow was lighter on the flagstone that led up to the doors from the concrete driveway beyond. Once perhaps instead of concrete the drive had been covered with brick, or even cobblestone. Regardless, Marie-Thérèse led the way, taking one of the large brass door handles in hand. She gazed down at it and caught with some surprise in her eye the letter "I" on each of the door handles. *« Interesante, »* she muttered.

She pulled on the right door's handle, listening to the hinges creak open. Inside the carriage house she could see a large hall, bathed in sunlight, that seemed cold to her sight. Nevertheless, she entered, and was astonished to find the hall warm, a fire crackling in a hearth somewhere not far from her. She was unsure where it was but was sure that was what she heard. Erasmus followed, wanting to retire from the snow for a few moments and enjoy what he was sure would be a warm room and perhaps even a nice cup of tea.

Marie-Thérèse walked further in, small flakes of snow flicking off of her boots with each step. Erasmus clombered on behind her, the thick snowpack on the bottoms of his boots leaving great tracks of the white stuff sprayed across the wooden floor.

The hall seemed empty, eerily so. Marie-Thérèse noticed, and felt a chill run up the back of her neck, "Where is everyone?" she asked.

Erasmus looked about and saw to his astonishment a flyer in a stand next to one of the entryways to the corridors that lay on either side of the hall. "I don't know. It says there's supposed to be a wedding in here today?"

"When?"

"At eleven."

Marie-Thérèse looked down at her watch, 10:00. "Where is everyone? There are always people at a wedding before time."

Erasmus looked up, starting to put together what he was thinking, "Hey, M.-T., why's it so cold in here?"

« Sais pas »[22]

Out of the corner of his eye, Erasmus saw a little girl, pigtails in her hair, an old white dress going down to her knees and black leather Mary Janes strapped above her stockings on her feet. "Look, there's someone!" he pointed.

Marie-Thérèse turned about, gazing towards the empty floor where Erasmus was pointing. "What do you mean?"

Erasmus was astounded, *« Cette fille, c'est là-bas, »*[23] he pointed again toward the empty floorboards. *« Ne vois-tu ci ?»*

« Rien, » Marie-Thérèse replied, her eyes wiedening.

The little girl was sitting on the floor, her legs not quite crossed, playing with an unseen toy in front of the fire. Erasmus walked up behind her, "Hello there," he started, a gentleness masking the building fear in his voice, "what are you playing with there?"

---

[22] "Don't know."
[23] "That girl, she's over there!"

"My horse," the girl replied in a voice eerily familiar. Marie-Thérèse jumped at the sound of what appeared to her to be a disembodied voice.

"What's your horse's name?" Erasmus asked.

"Edie," the little one replied, not looking up from her toy, still unseen from Erasmus's vantage behind her.

"My name's Erasmus–"

"It's a pleasure to meet you, Mr. Erasmus," the girl said.

"What's your name?" Erasmus asked, walking around her so that he could see her face in profile, though masked by the flickering embers of the fire before her.

"Honoria," she replied, looking up at Erasmus for the first time. A shock of horror filled his heart as his eyes caught those radiant blue orbs. he felt cold and looked on in amazement as little Honoria disappeared before his eyes.

"Did–, did she say, 'Honoria'?" Marie-Thérèse stuttered.

"It sounded like it," Erasmus replied, not entirely sure what had just happened.

"Was that a ghost?"

Erasmus looked over at Marie-Thérèse, "M.T., she had Mrs. Inkpenne's eyes!"

~

Erasmus and Marie-Thérèse were still in a state of shock when they returned to the barn two hours later at noon. Erasmus was less sure of what he'd seen than he had ever been before. The evidence pointed to something that didn't make sense. With this insecurity, he found himself standing in front of the barn once again, with Marie-Thérèse by his side. Bill Doty had readied the horses, and a pair of some of the strongest steeds Erasmus had ever seen stood before them. These weren't like the carriage horses in Central Park or on the Plaza in Kansas City. Their legs and hooves were thicker, stronger than either of those, or even than the war horses that served as mounts for the Household Cavalry in London. These great draughthorses were just the animals needed for the task of pulling a fine old sleigh like the one Bill Doty brought forward from the barn.

"Alright, up you two go," he said, standing alongside the sleigh, its door ajar for the two lovers to board. Marie-Thérèse went first, with a graceful hand from Bill, followed by Erasmus, who also got help from the stable hand and coachman.

Bill Doty leaped up into his seat and taking the reins in hand he cracked their leather bands, sending the draughthorses forward in equal step. "These are two of my strongest horses," he said, leaning back to look at his passengers, "John and Quincy, they're brothers, five years old, and always happy to go for a ride."

"Fitting New England names," Erasmus called back over the increasingly loud sleighs that rubbed against the hard ground.

"After two of our finest presidents," Bill shouted back, the sound of the runners growing as they left the snow-covered grass in front of the barn for the hard concrete of the Inn's main drive. After a minute they turned off of the drive and, quickly crossing catty-corner over the road that ran past the inn on its western side, they came to an old dirt track through the forest.

The scenery of the woods seemed to fly by them, the horses pulling the sleigh at a good pace across the snow-covered grass. Erasmus felt the breeze blow through across his face and looked over to see Marie-Thérèse's hair blowing about, some strands in her face, others soaring with the breeze back from her head, still more finding contact with the wool of her hat. Erasmus leaned over to her and brushed some of the hair away from her cheeks. She turned to look at him, smiling graciously. She held up her hand and stroked his face, the leather of her gloves feeling unusual to him. Still he leaned in and kissed her on the cheek, watching as her pale frozen cheeks glowed red at his kiss. She kissed him back, this time upon his lips, and felt the soft embrace of his lips upon hers, their love overwhelming the coldness that they felt.

Bill let the horses take a slower pace, lessening the breeze and allowing the soft sounds of the forest to come through over the sleighs rubbing against the snow. "Are you on vacation here?"

"Yeah, just a week away," Erasmus replied.

"Where are you coming from, then?"

"New York," Erasmus replied.

"That's a big place!" Bill replied, "too big for my liking."

"Are you from here then?"

"Jackson? Yeah, I've lived her my whole life."

There was a pause. Erasmus thought for a moment, "Have you heard of anything unusual happening in the carriage house?"

"The carriage house? O, sure! There's that little girl.

"Was she playing with a toy horse?"

"Yeah, in front of the fireplace in the great hall.

"That's the one," Bill replied, pulling the reins slightly to the left to keep John and Quincy on track.

"She said her name was Honoria," Erasmus noted.

"O, so she told you her name then? Well, that's a first that I've heard," Bill replied, leaning back and taking a quick swig of the coffee that he'd left behind him.

"Who was she?"

"A little girl," Bill replied authoritatively.

"I know, but what sort of girl is she?"

"What do you think?" he asked.

"A ghost?"

"Well done," Bill replied, cracking the whip.

"So, she is a ghost!" Marie-Thérèse cried, "then why didn't I see her?"

"She only appears to some people and not others. I've seen her, as has most of the staff in the spa in that building. But Mrs. Inkpenne, she's never seen that little girl."

"Then, could the little girl be a young Mrs. Inkpenne?!" Mari-Thérèse shouted over the sleigh.

"Yeah, it's possible, "Bill commented, bringing the carriage to.

"But how is that possible?" Marie-Thérèse asked.

"I don't know, but there's always been something about Mrs. Inkpenne. I'm sure you've noticed it too. Something strange."

"But how can there be a ghost of a living person?"

"There's the conundrum," Erasmus commented.

Marie-Thérèse thought about it, "If Mrs. Inkpenne is alive but you've seen the ghost of her youth, then was it really a ghost?"

"I don't know, I haven't really seen any ghosts before."

"I've seen a few, but only in certain places. That carriage house is one. It's always that little girl or her mother, a tall, dignified woman, wearing some sort of dress out of a Sherlock Holmes story," Bill replied.

"How old is Mrs. Inkpenne?" Erasmus asked, his mind racing between thoughts.

"I don't know," Bill replied, "it's not a question you ask a lady."

Erasmus looked over at Marie-Thérèse, "It's true," she replied.

"But if Mrs. Inkpenne's mother is wearing those sorts of clothes then she must be very old!" Erasmus mused aloud.

"But, she doesn't look it." said Bill.

"Something here doesn't make sense."

"Yeah, I don't ask questions anymore, it's just confusing, and there don't really seem to be any answers," Bill replied, snapping the reins and sending John and Quincy the horses forward once more.

The sleigh glided across the snowpack along a hillside path. The way felt worn down, as if well used since before the colonial days. Erasmus let his questions about Mrs. Inkpenne stay behind him and leaned back in the sleigh, leaning close in towards Marie-Thérèse. They held each other's hands tightly and watched as the scenery flew on by them.

The sleigh was an old vehicle, made of a darkly stained wood. It was like many an old-fashioned carriage, yet instead of wheels it had what seemed like a cross of ice skates and skis on its rails, allowing it to glide across the snow in a way that no carriage could. It was the perfect way to travel about the White Mountains in winter, Erasmus concluded, especially before the roads were paved and cars had been invented.

Erasmus noticed as they began to turn, the Sun moving in its position above their heads. "Are we going back to the Inn?"

"Yeah, it looks like Quincy is in need of a nap," Bill sighed.

"Already?" Marie-Thérèse retorted, surprised at Bill's assessment.

"He's a sleepy fellow for sure."

"Better than a sleepy hollow," Erasmus joked, to Marie-Thérèse's discomfort. He noted her concerned look, "Don't worry, if there's a headless horseman in these woods, we'll probably see it before we head back to New York."

"That's not making it any better, Erasmus," she irritably shot back, folding her arms across her chest and leaning away from him.

Erasmus realised his mistake, "I'm sorry, M.T."

"All this talk of ghosts is unsettling me," she replied.

"But if they're dead, then they can't hurt you, right?"

"But what if they're not dead?"

7

Mrs. Inkpenne

That evening and the following day went relatively quietly for both Erasmus and Marie-Thérèse. They had enjoyed their brisk ride in Bill Doty's sleigh, and had especially enjoyed helping Bill feed John and Quincy afterwards in their stalls in the inn's stable. Erasmus drew the raised eyebrows of Marie-Thérèse by making a Nativity joke, after laying an especially large bundle of hay into a manger in John's stall. She enjoyed his jokes, but not nearly as much as he would have liked. That evening they dined, and not drinking quite as much wine as the evening prior, they were able to remember the rest of the night, which was spent largely in their room watching the best that the local public television station had to offer.

On Tuesday morning, Erasmus woke earlier than he had planned. He wasn't sure why, he hadn't had any bad dreams, and didn't feel terribly hungry. Nevertheless, the pall of sleep had left his eyes, and he felt ready to go down to the dining room and see what was what. Without checking the clock, Erasmus made his way into the lavatory, showered, shaved, and dressed quickly, donning the same old yellow sweater that he had worn since leaving New York on Sunday morning. However, not looking closely enough at what clothes he was taking from the dresser, he inadvertently grabbed a pair of plus fours, golfing knee-breeches, that Marie-Thérèse must have brought. Not knowing her to be much of a golfer, Erasmus was vexed by the sudden appearance of such a fine pair of bottoms, but nevertheless decided to don them for at least the morning. As he left the room and made his way down the stair, thinking to himself an old vaudeville tune that had been played on the piano the evening before at dinner, Erasmus strolled into the dining room to find it empty save one chair. The room was dark, save the light from an old oil lamp that illuminated a table near the dining room.

Mrs. Inkpenne, sitting with her back to Erasmus, set down a teacup that she'd been holding, placing it onto its saucer on the table before her. "You're early, Mr. Plumwood. Breakfast doesn't begin for another two hours."

"O! Is that the time?" Erasmus started, looking at his wristwatch, which he'd inadvertently left on his bedside upstairs.

Mrs. Inkpenne turned about and faced Erasmus, "Is there something that I can help you with?"

"O, no, nothing. Just couldn't sleep anymore. Thought I'd come downstairs for a bit of a stroll."

"Sleep," the innkeeper muttered.

"What's that?"

"Nothing the mind, Mr. Plumwood," she snapped back.

Erasmus began to turn to go, figuring it'd be better if he just went back upstairs and read a book, or perhaps sat in the living room in front of the fire to read. Maybe they'd have a copy of the paper already from Conway, or even the latest morning edition from New York lying about there. But something about Mrs. Inkpenne stopped him. For the first time since he'd known her, she didn't seem as stern, as fearsome. Granted, she was still awfully cold, and her gaze scared him to no end, but something about her still made him curious.

"Em, Mrs. Inkpenne, could I sit with you for a while? Only I don't want to wake Marie-Thérèse, and I'm not entirely sure what to do this early in the morning."

"You may," she replied, motioning towards an empty chair beside her own.

Erasmus stepped forward, the floorboards creaking beneath his feet. He pulled the old wooden chair back and sat down in it gently, not wanting to upset Mrs. Inkpenne, who frankly he feared more than most people, about as much as the man who liked to bring his ferrets into the café at 78th and Amsterdam Ave. Erasmus never liked ferrets.

Mrs. Inkpenne was a tad ferretish, tall, slender, with a pronounced nose, not unlike a certain M.P. from Berkshire at the time of writing, who may or may not have been leader of the Tories for terribly long after a rather substantial vote was cast one year prior to Erasmus's and Marie-Thérèse's visit to the Noel Inn.

Mrs. Inkpenne peered at Erasmus's face through the dark. "There's something elegant about your features, Mr. Plumwood. Are you English?"

"My mother's family is."

"Where from?"

"London."

"A beautiful city. I remember it when King Edward was on the throne. Even New York couldn't compare to the grandeur of London."

"King Edward?" Erasmus asked, trying to imagine how Depression-era London could've been called grand.

"Yes, and what a man he was. I met him not long after he succeeded to the throne."

"Where are you from, Mrs. Inkpenne?" Erasmus asked.

"Right here, in Conway. My family owned the house at the top of the hill."

"It looks like a beautiful house," Erasmus replied, setting a hand down on the table.

"It was full of life once. My sisters and I loved to play there with our cousins."

"How many sisters do you have?"

"There were four of us. All of them have long since died."

"I'm sorry to hear that," Erasmus replied. "Do you have any family left today?"

"No. My sister Ethel had a son, but he died in the War, killed in a far-off land. They buried him there, my nephew Randolph. His mother never saw him again."

"That's so sad," Erasmus whispered, watching on as Mrs. Inkpenne showed the first bit of emotion in a long while. "Do you miss him?" he asked.

Mrs. Inkpenne sighed, taking a sip of her tea, "O, not as much anymore. It's been so long. I miss my cousins more, they were a wild bunch. They'd come up here every year or so from New York to visit. I went down to see them too once, at their house on Long Island. We had such fun together. My cousin Eleanor, now she was the one to watch out for. The leader of the pack."

"That's a beautiful name, Eleanor," Erasmus replied.

"Yes, she was a charming woman, full of life, and full of compassion for the poor too. She had a look in her eye that'd make anyone stop what they were doing and pay attention to her."

"What happened to her?" Erasmus asked, feeling more comfortable to be direct with the innkeeper.

Mrs. Inkpenne was taken off guard by this question, "What happened? Not all of my family died in far off wars, Mr. Plumwood."

"I'm sorry, Mrs. Inkpenne, I didn't mean to be rude."

Mrs. Inkpenne sighed, "Well, she became quite famous, mostly thanks to her husband. I didn't see much of her after she married. They moved to Washington. He was a bureaucrat, working long hours for the Federal Government."

"Do you remember what he did?"

"That's not important. He was always a bit headstrong, Eleanor's husband. I never liked him as much. They would send me a Christmas card each year. It'd normally arrive today. Eleanor would always write it by hand, asking after me. Every year she would say how much she wanted to come and visit me at the Inn. But she never came. Not even after her husband died. I suppose she was always too busy, you see once she became a widow, she started to work for herself, doing the things that she loved."

"She sounds like quite an amazing woman."

"O, she was. So elegant, so refined, and so very intelligent. I haven't met anyone quite like her until I met your *copine* Madame Merlinais."

Erasmus smiled a large giddy smile, "We're dating now, since Sunday."

Mrs. Inkpenne gazed back into his eyes, the cold blue seemed to soften just a little bit. "You are a good couple. Do you plan to marry her?"

Erasmus was taken aback, "Marry? Um, maybe but I don't know how long we'll be a couple. You see, I'm moving to San Francisco after Christmas. She still has another semester at Columbia before she finishes."

"So, then you'll have four months apart, four months is not that long, Mr. Plumwood. I've seen many more months than that."

"But what if she falls in love with another man or even a woman?"

"Then perhaps it wasn't meant to be."

Erasmus looked on at Mrs. Inkpenne, shocked at that, "But if it wasn't meant to be then why do we make such a good couple."

"Mr. Plumwood, there have been many good couples who don't marry. Sometimes that is how life takes its course. Remember that we can't predict the future, only estimate where it will lead us."

"But we have free will, my mother always says that, we have free will, and so we can decide our futures."

"Yes, but we cannot control the wills of others. If we could Eleanor would have come here every year. If we could my nephew Randolph wouldn't have died so far from home. If we could then this world would not be as beautiful of a place. Remember, the cost of liberty is uncertainty, but isn't it better to be uncertain about the future than to be a slave to someone else's will?"

"That sounds like John and Quincy," Erasmus joked. Mrs. Inkpenne's eyes glowed blue with irritation, "The presidents, ma'am, not the horses."

Mrs. Inkpenne's eyes calmed again. Erasmus could tell she was not pleased with his jokes; *"granted,"* Erasmus thought, *"it'd be hard to please most people with my jokes these days."*

"How long has your family owned this inn?" Erasmus asked, attempting to break the re-frozen ice once again.

"My ancestors built it when they first came here from England. We come from old Kentish stock. It has been in the family ever since."

"That's quite the story," Erasmus replied, amazed at how long her family had been there in Jackson.

"Yes, it has been quite a while. My great-grandfather was just over there in the parlour when the Redcoats stayed here."

"Your great-grandfather? During the Revolution?"

"Yes, he was five at the time. At dinner he served them ale and then after dinner once they'd gone to bed, he ran into the village to get the local patriot militia. They came in and killed every last English officer who was drinking in this very room. All but one, one who begged for his life, for the sake of his new-born son."

"What happened to him?" Erasmus leaned forward in his chair.

"The patriots let that soldier go. He ran away, all the way back to Montréal. He told them about how ferocious the mountain men of New Hampshire were, and the British never came back, at least until the War of 1812. But here's where I am curious, Mr. Plumwood. Because my great-grandfather drew a sketch of that soldier from memory when he was an old man, around the time of the Gold Rush in California. I have that sketch hanging on the wall in the parlour. Do you want to go see it?"

Erasmus was uncertain where this was going, but agreed nevertheless to go with the innkeeper, "Sure, this is a neat story."

Mrs. Inkpenne rose from her chair, her heels struck the floor with quite the resounding clop. She led Erasmus through a side door near the piano into an antechamber where some children's toys were housed. There she turned the corner and walked into the parlour, the embers of last night's fire glowing in reminiscence in the fireplace. She led him to a framed picture on the wall facing the dining room. "Here he is, George Burgheley, the survivor. He was a lieutenant in the King's Army at the time, though I don't know what happened to him from there."

Erasmus stared at that face, so eerily similar to his own. He knew the rest of the story, "George was sent home in 1777, his service in the American Colonies was deemed complete. He returned to his home on Minories in London to his wife Cecily and their infant son William."

Mrs. Inkpenne gazed into Erasmus's eyes, "You have his face, that's for certain. You have the same face. But your eyes are different; familiar yet different."

"That'll be the Darwin side in me."

"Darwin?" she asked, raising an eyebrow.

"Yes, that's where I got my name. I was named for my second great-grandfather, Erasmus Burgheley, who was named for his grandfather Erasmus Darwin.'"

"You come from quite the family, Mr. Plumwood."

"Thank you, Mrs. Inkpenne." He thought about it, dared to say it, "And it sounds like you do as well."

"I don't know about that, we're just simple innkeepers in northern New Hampshire," she muttered.

"How many families can say they have owned the same establishment since before the Revolution?"

"Mr. Plumwood, few, but that isn't something to brag about. Longevity is just as much a curse as it is a blessing. We've been lucky to have this sort of history, but that luck is not always a good thing."

"I don't understand," Erasmus replied, looking down at Mrs. Inkpenne's purple skirts.

"You are still young, you don't know what it means to be old, to lose so many of the people that you love."

Erasmus felt ashamed, "I'm sorry, ma'am, I didn't mean to intrude."

Mrs. Inkpenne observed his apologetics and felt kinder in her heart for him. "Mr. Plumwood, I'm sorry for my curtness."

Erasmus felt relieved, a burden rising off of his chest. "Mrs. Inkpenne, could I ask you an odd question?"

"Haven't you already?"

He nodded, "Do you believe in ghosts?"

Mrs. Inkpenne stopped and looked at the phantom glow of the embers in the fire. "Ghosts are all around us, Mr. Plumwood. They come both as memories and as inventions of our imaginations."

"Have you seen a ghost?"

She looked off at the windows of the inn, the glow of the lights on the front porch contrasting with the pitch blackness of the northern winter's night. "Sometimes, when I sit in the dining room late at night in February, I will find myself surrounded by those British officers. They'll drink from their tankards and talk about their wives and sweethearts back home in England, they'll groan about the cold weather here in America, and about the French back in Canada, but often it'll just be them and me. Then I'll see my great-grandfather, the young boy of five, quietly leaving out the front door of the inn, running down the steps to go down the road and warn the patriots. Whether their souls are still here, in the place where they were murdered, I don't know. It could well just be my imagination of an old family story that my grandfather used to tell me."

"There were ghosts in my grandfather's house," Erasmus replied, leaning against the wall near his ancestor's portrait, "on Russell Square. I was sure of it. That house had so many nooks in it, so many small places where things had been left behind or hidden. I remember one day when I found my second great-grandfather Erasmus's beaver skin top hat. It was in an old wardrobe in the attic. I tried it on for size and was startled to see the reflection of an old man in a black frock coat with white hair and a white moustache staring at me. I was sure it was him, still wandering the attic of that old house."

"Christmas is a time for ghosts, remember that. There are so many memories associated with this season, it could drive the paranoid mad," Mrs. Inkpenne replied. She noticed out the porch windows the first rays of the morning Sun rising over the mountains. Mrs. Inkpenne went to work, opening the fireplace grate and setting four logs in there, chopped out in the yard near the barn by Bill Doty sometime before. She then took a match from the mantle and lit the fire once again. The embers reignited, and revived with the vigour of a tiger, not tamed but caged, forced to do humanity's bidding. "It's morning," she said. "I'd better get to work. Breakfast won't cook itself, Mr. Plumwood."

Erasmus smiled, and nodded as Mrs. Inkpenne turned, walking past the registration desk and back into the dining room. Erasmus stood there, looking into the eyes of his ancestor, the only survivor of what was surely a massacre that had to have turned heads in London. He'd known about it for a long while, since his grandfather told him the story on a trip to the National Portrait Gallery. In one room there were paintings of George Washington, Benjamin Franklin on one level, and Lord Cornwallis on another above them. Erasmus thought it odd that Cornwallis was higher up than Washington, despite the latter's victory over the former at Yorktown. The Revolution had always been a touchy topic when Erasmus and his parents had been over for dinner at Russell Square with his grandfather Arthur. A devoted royalist, Arthur Burgheley said there were three events in English history that changed things for the worst, "firstly the execution of Sir Thomas More, secondly Oliver Cromwell, and thirdly the American Revolution."

Erasmus remembered him saying, "We are so alike, America and Britain, if only we could be a part of the same family like we are with Canada, Australia, and New Zealand."

Erasmus smiled at the thought of his grandfather referring to him and his father as "wayward colonials," especially after one dinner when the conversation became so focused on the Revolution now long passed that Erasmus's father Charles Plumwood had stood up, during Arthur's toast to the Queen, and after the wine was drunk for Her Majesty, proceeded to propose a toast to "all those brave American patriots who sacrificed their lives for the cause of liberty against a tyrannical King!" Arthur sat there, as Erasmus remembered, at the head of the table silently as Charles, slightly tipsy from too much Bordeaux, began to sing his favourite verse from "Yankee Doodle" at full voice about one Continental soldier's large musket:

> *And when they went and fired it off*
> *It took a horn of powder*
> *It made a noise like father's gun*
> **Only a nation louder!**

Charles loved to shout that last line. The following evening, Arthur ensured his daughter Helvetica restrict her husband, his *colonial* son-in-law to just two glasses of Bordeaux instead of the four that he'd consumed the night prior.

Erasmus smiled, he hadn't seen his parents in four months, not since he was last in Kansas City with Marie-Thérèse in August. Normally they'd try to come to New York once in the Autumn to visit, but this year his mother's teaching schedule wouldn't allow it. The fear of losing her post as an Assistant Professor in the History Department at the local university due to budget cuts from on high was a constant fear, and she had more than once discussed moving into her father's old house at Russell Square with Charles, who despite having worked for nigh thirty years at the same mapmakers on Main Street in Downtown Kansas City, was open to the idea of moving away, starting fresh and new in London. "They'll always need cartographers," he had said.

"I wonder if I might end up back in London," Erasmus said to his sixth great-grandfather's portrait.

"You're a dual citizen, you have every right to move there," Marie-Thérèse replied, having just come down the stairs. "I was wondering where you were. Couldn't sleep?"

"Yeah, it was one of those early mornings," Erasmus replied.

Marie-Thérèse walked up to his side, and looked intently at the portrait, "I didn't know you were a sketch artist?"

"I'm not," Erasmus replied, raising an eyebrow at his friend.

"Then who did this portrait of you?"

"Mrs. Inkpenne's great-grandfather."

Marie-Thérèse's mouth made words but no sound uttered from within. She stammered, "Ghosts yesterday, time travel today? There's something strange about this place."

"There is, but that's not me. That's my sixth great-grandfather George Burgheley."

"Wait, why is there a portrait of your sixth great-grandfather on the wall here? You're not somehow related to Mrs. Inkpenne, are you? A long lost third cousin?"

"Not as far as I know, but her family's from Kent, so I wouldn't put it past that."

Marie-Thérèse put her hands on her hips.

"My sixth great-grandfather came here in 1776 during the Revolution. He was a lieutenant in the British Army. Mrs. Inkpenne's great-grandfather told the local patriots about the British officers drinking in this inn, and they came and killed all of them except old George here."

"So, you're saying that your sixth great-grandfather stayed here? And he was the only guest that night that didn't die? That's reassuring."

"I'll admit, it's not a pleasing story when you put it that way."

Marie-Thérèse laughed a hollow laugh, consumed more with fear than drollness.

"Do you want to get breakfast?" Erasmus asked, motioning toward the dining room on the opposite side of the wall from them.

"Sure, but just two more questions," Marie-Thérèse replied hesitantly.

"Go ahead."

"Firstly, if Mrs. Inkpenne's great-grandfather was alive during the American Revolution, how old do you think she is?"

"I don't know, it's not a polite question to ask."

"Fair enough."

"What's the second question?" Erasmus asked, wondering somewhat hopefully where this was going.

"Why are you wearing my plus fours?"

Erasmus looked down, sure enough they were rather small on him, and the soft paisley pattern defined the shape of his thigh quite well. "O, I'm sorry, I must have put these on by accident when I was getting dressed at four o' clock."

Marie-Thérèse looked his legs up and down, she stepped forward and leaned in close to him, "They suit you."

Erasmus smiled, and kissed her cheek. She blushed a little but smiled with a far bigger grin.

Erasmus knew that he loved her, and Marie-Thérèse knew that she loved him. The only question in his mind was whether or not that love could be sustained across four months and 4,600 km. The only question in her mind, only beginning to percolate, was if, or when he would propose. « *Nous avons beaucoup de temps, mais un paradis d'hiver est un bon lieu pour une demande du mariage,* »[24] she thought.

---

[24] *"We have lots of time, but a winter paradise is a good place for a proposal."*

8

Waltzing Matilda

"So, are you sure that your brother Charles isn't a nut?" Erasmus asked, taking a bite of a small tea biscuit that had been left in their room by the staff.

"What do you mean 'a nut?' Yes, he's a bit crazy, but I wouldn't call him a nut."

"If you say so."

"I mean, he did once eat moose steak –"

"Moose steak?!"

"Yeah, he was on a hunting trip in Northern Québec with his university friends. He said that was all that was available."

Erasmus's face morphed into a look of disgust, "That's horrible!"

"What's the difference between eating moose and eating beef?" Marie-Thérèse asked.

"We raise the cows to be eaten. Moose aren't like that. They're wild, and majestic, and have some great mating calls."

Marie-Thérèse rolled her eyes at the last moose superlative. "They're aggressive animals though. They'll charge you and intend to kill you."

"Yeah, but that's what makes them fun," Erasmus quipped.

"I don't think I'd call death by moose fun."

"No, but it does sound rather funny you'll admit."

"O will I?"

Erasmus noted his verbal misstep, "Perhaps you will, perhaps you won't."

"What's the most outrageous thing that you've eaten, Erasmus?"

"Besides the dirt every time that I fall over?"

"Besides that, that's almost an extra food group for you."

Erasmus chuckled, "I'd say horse."

Now Marie-Thérèse was disgusted, "How could you eat a horse?"

"By accident, *ma chérie*. It was at a pub in Dover, right around when the English and Irish meatpacking plants mixed up the horse and cow meat back in 2013. Do you remember hearing about that?"

"Yes, your mother wouldn't stop talking about it on the phone."

"Right. Well, when I went over for my grandfather's funeral, I stayed on a little bit longer and went out to Kent with my parents to

104

visit Rochester, Canterbury, and Dover. My mother always liked Canterbury Cathedral, and my father and I enjoy visiting Rochester and Dover Castles. Anyway, so we stopped for lunch at a small roadside pub outside of Canterbury and ordered burgers. When the food came and we all quickly took bites out of our food and suddenly discovered to our horror that it wasn't beef, but something lankier, a more drawn out meat. My mother was the one who connected the dots. As we were looking at our burgers, trying to figure out what they were made of she let out a loud 'neeeigh!'"

"That's horrible," Marie-Thérèse said, setting down her cup of chocolat and looking at her boyfriend, *«Je s'ai embrassé un homme qui a mangé du cheval, »*[25] she thought in horror.

"Yeah, we didn't take another bite, just finished eating the fries and left."

Marie-Thérèse sat there thinking for a moment. She'd never heard of horse meat being described as *lanky*, though then again she'd never really considered horses as food.

"So, what's the craziest thing you've ever eaten?" Erasmus asked, turning the tables on his Canadian girlfriend.

"Does human count?" she asked.

"Excuse me?" Erasmus's mind began to race, *"Am I up for one of those relationships that began in a sweet embrace and ended up with one person in the couple being filleted, barbequed, and consumed with a large bottle of claret?"*

"I'm only joking," she said with a wicked grin. She leaned forward and gave him a light kiss on the lips.

"I like jokes, as you know," Erasmus began.

"Yes?"

"But cannibalism jokes aren't exactly my thing."

"But they're the juiciest," she retorted.

"Funny," Erasmus said, looking at her wearily.

As they talked a note slipped through below the door. Marie-Thérèse walked over to the door, leaned down and collected it in her hands.

"What is it?" Erasmus asked.

"It's an invitation to a waltz this evening."

"A waltz?"

"Yes, it's *A Waltz to Celebrate the arrival of the Ambassador of Australia Tonight*," Marie-Thérèse read.

"Why would they have a waltz for that?"

"I don't know, this is a pretty odd place, they seem to have special events for most things."

---

[25] "I've kissed a man who's eaten horse."

"Fair enough. Is there a dress code?"

Marie-Thérèse looked at the rest of the invitation, which she had extracted from a crisp white paper envelope. "It says 'black tie is preferred. We will be celebrating our first diplomatic guests since the Revolution," Erasmus raised an eyebrow as Marie-Thérèse continued, "please come dressed formally."

"Should I go and warn the Ambassador what happened the last time a Servant of the Crown came to visit this inn?" Erasmus joked.

"You should certainly introduce yourself to him when we go down."

"Why?"

"He's an ambassador. I bet he knows a lot of people."

"Himmler knew a lot of people, it doesn't mean I would've wanted to meet him."

Marie-Thérèse caught the rich sarcasm in his voice. "Don't worry, I'm sure he'll be friendly. He's Australian."

"Have you been to Australia?" Erasmus asked, giving his eyebrows a work out yet again.

"No, have you?"

"No."

"Why'd you ask?"

"Just checking."

"Erasmus, what's gotten into you today?"

"You made a joke about wanting to eat me just a few minutes ago."

"A joke, Erasmus, a joke, though I admit it wasn't in the best taste, I mean there's not much meat on your bones."

"Look who's talking," Erasmus retorted.

Marie-Thérèse stopped for a moment and stared at him.

"I just put my foot in my mouth, didn't I?" Erasmus said hesitantly, recognizing his mistake.

"You could say that."

"I'm sorry, M.T. How can I make this up to you?"

Marie-Thérèse thought for a moment, "Help me pick out my outfit for the waltz tonight."

Erasmus smiled faintly, "Okay then."

He stood and walked over to the closet where she had hung up her dresses. Opening the mirrored door, he rifled through them gently, choosing a very elegant grey garment with light blue highlights. Its skirt was a little pencilish, but not terribly so. "How about this?"

Marie-Thérèse looked it over, "Yes, good choice. And the shoes?"

Erasmus looked down at the bottom of the closet, "You really did bring four pairs of shoes," he said in astonishment at the sight of two pairs of heels, one with a higher eight to nine-centimetre heel, a pair of blue flats, and her blue suede riding boots that she'd worn for most of the time outdoors on this trip.

"I'm always prepared for any occasion."

"Fair enough," he said. He picked a pair of blue leather heels that had a decent height to them. "How about these?"

"Those'll work with the dress. And a coat?"

Erasmus looked next to the dresses at the coats that she'd brought, "How about this one? With the blue on it?"

"I'll be a blue winter queen by the looks of it," Marie-Thérèse replied.

"Is that a bad thing?" Erasmus asked, holding the coat by its hanger before him, half turned out from the closet, his eyes looking into hers.

"No, it's elegant."

"O good," Erasmus replied, breathing a sigh of relief. He laid the coat down on Marie-Thérèse's bed and went to go sit down again.

"We're not done," she said pointedly, "You haven't picked out my jewellery yet."

Erasmus looked over at the jewellery box on the top of the dresser. Stepping over to it, he opened the box and looked at what was available. "Earrings?"

"Sure."

"Necklace?"

"Of course."

"Bracelets?"

"Okay, how about these?" Erasmus asked, taking a pair of earrings in the shape of twin ornamental seals dangling from silver bands.

"O, those are fun! My mother got those for me in San Francisco."

Erasmus set them on the dresser top. He then turned to the necklaces, picking a gold one with an ornamental lily on it, "And this?"

"Sure, that'll keep with the aquatic theme."

Next to the bracelets, where he chose a simple silver band, looking it over he noticed that engraved into its inner ring was a beautifully carved French phrase, « *Je t'aime.* »[26]

"*Perfect,*" he thought, turning to hand it to Marie-Thérèse, "How about this one, *mon amour?* »

She took it in hand and looked it over, quickly catching the French inside of it, "O yes," she said with a great smile. She stood and hugged Erasmus, kissing him, « *Ce sont tous des bonnes options* »[27] she whispered into his ear.

---

[26] "I love you."

« *Je t'aime, Marie-Thérèse Merlinais,* » Erasmus whispered back. He kissed her in return and thought of nothing else but the love in his arms.

She leaned on his shoulder, "I'm going to miss you."

Erasmus silently hugged her, knowing what he wanted to say but unable to say it. He had a golden opportunity, a dream job lined up for him, but his life was here with Marie-Thérèse, in her arms. "We should probably get dressed," he said.

"Yes," she stepped back and took her clothes and jewellery into the lavatory.

Erasmus stood there in the bedroom, the lavatory door closed, the woman he loved on the other side. "It's only four months," he muttered, "Just four months. The Bay Area's a big place, she's bound to find a job out there."

As he could hear Marie-Thérèse dressing behind the door, he went to the closet and noted his nicer suit, which she'd brought, knowing he would forget it. It was crisp, a deep black in colour, with the cleanest white shirt imaginable. Erasmus took off his black everyday trousers, yellow sweater, and blue shirt and quickly attached the suspenders to the black suit trousers. He pulled the trousers up his legs and let the suspenders slide into place over his shoulders before remembering that he should have put his shirt on first. Quickly lowering the suspenders, he attempted to put the shirt on while holding his trousers in place, but found the latter sliding down his legs, as he knew they probably would. Erasmus figured the best course of action to do would just be to put the shirt on and not worry about the trousers, but to make sure he didn't rip them, which would be problematic. Sliding his arms down the sleeves, he buttoned the shirt up and leaned over to grab his trousers, losing his balance and falling on his head. As he lay there, practically kowtowing to whatever it was in front of him, his weight pressed down on the crown of his head and his kneecaps, he heard the lavatory door open.

Marie-Thérèse stood there, Erasmus figured she must look stunning, but at that moment in time he couldn't see much save the carpet. "What happened to you?" she asked, trying hard not to laugh.

"I fell."

"I see that. How'd it happen?"

"I was trying to pull my trousers up from my ankles and I lost my balance."

"Are you sure you don't just fall over every time you get confused?"

"Do I look like a fainting goat?"

---

[27] "These are all good options."

Marie-Thérèse looked him up and down, "Well, now that you say it…"

"Funny," Erasmus said, falling onto his left side and rolling so he could push himself up.

"You really are an odd man, Erasmus Plumwood."

"Better an odd man than an odd frog."

"I'm not even going to ask," she said, leaning over and helping him pull his trousers up.

"You don't have to," Erasmus said.

"I think I might, just this one time. You seem a bit confused today."

"I think I'm always confused."

Erasmus took the suspenders from her hands and let them snap back up onto his shoulders, this time atop his shirt. He then took the black bowtie in hand that went with this suit and walked over to the mirror. "Now here comes the tricky bit," he muttered.

Erasmus attempted to tie it, but quickly found himself overly confused again. Marie-Thérèse stepped forward to help, but Erasmus turned her away, "No. Let me do this myself."

"Okay," she said, stepping back a bit.

Erasmus closed his eyes and let his fingers do the work, tying it perfectly, even adding a little flourish at the end, much to Marie-Thérèse's delight.

Reopening his eyes, he found Marie-Thérèse behind him, holding his suitcoat open, ready for him to don, *"Merci,"* he said, smiling as she slid it up his arms.

There they stood together, Erasmus Plumwood and Marie-Thérèse Merlinais, decked out in their finest. They looked at each other in the mirror, awestruck at how lucky they both were. Erasmus looked at the clock on the bedside table, "It's six, let's go down."

"Okay," she smiled.

~

The Noel Inn appeared slightly different, a tad crisper, livelier than it had been before. The twenty or so guests were all in their finery, the women in beautiful dresses of a wide array of colours, the men in their black evening suits with crisp black bowties. Some of the men wore military medals on their chests, though they were few and far between. The only person who hadn't changed a bit was Mrs. Inkpenne, who stood off from the side of the action, watching intently as her guests mingled in the parlour. At the centre of it all was a tall slender man, with soft blond hair, pale skin, and bright blue eyes. His evening suit was especially well pressed, his medals reflecting the embers of the fire about the room in a way that made it look like whosever ghosts dwelled in the place were dancing in light.

Marie-Thérèse led Erasmus to the centre of the room where the ambassador stood, walking right up to him with a smile on her face, "Good evening, Ambassador Lawrence."

"Good evening," he replied, "Do I know you?"

"Yes, we met about five years ago when you were posted to Ottawa. I'm Monsieur Merlinais's daughter, Marie-Thérèse."

« O oui, Madame Merlinais, enchantée, et qui est votre ami ?»[28]

Marie-Thérèse turned to Erasmus, "This is my boyfriend, Erasmus Plumwood."

"A pleasure to meet you, Mr. Plumwood."

"The same, Ambassador."

"What brings you to this side of the border?" the Ambassador asked Marie-Thérèse.

"O, Erasmus and I live in New York. We're just up here on holiday."

"That's nice, are you enjoying it so far?"

"Yes, I think so. This is a very lovely little inn," Erasmus replied.

The Ambassador smiled, then turned to Marie-Thérèse, "Can I ask you a question?"

"Of course."

"What do you make of the innkeeper?"

"She's an odd person for sure, there's something that doesn't make sense about her," Marie-Thérèse replied.

"She looks like she's dressed from 1914 or thereabouts," he noted, quickly looking over toward the innkeeper who was standing past the stairway leading up to the bedchambers.

"That's only the start of it," Erasmus said, leaping into the conversation, "She told me yesterday morning that her great-grandfather was a boy during the American Revolution."

"Her great-grandfather? But either her parents were very old when she was born or she's older than she looks," the Ambassador thought aloud yet softly to the three of them.

"If you want to know more about the place, talk to Bill Doty, he's the stable hand. He's been here all his life," Marie-Thérèse suggested.

"I'll do that. This could be a good mystery for my holiday."

"How long are you here?"

---

[28] "O yes, Madame Merlinais, it's good to meet you, and who is your friend?"

"Through Christmas," the Ambassador replied. "My wife and children like to get away from Washington when we can. It's not really our favourite city to spend Christmas in."

"That's understandable," Erasmus replied, thinking about how annoying it'd be to be stuck in D.C. on the one day a year when the Smithsonian was closed.

"When do you leave?" the Ambassador asked, changing the subject slightly.

"Tomorrow morning. Erasmus is moving later this week," Marie-Thérèse added.

"O yeah, where to?"

"San Francisco," Erasmus replied softly.

"It's beautiful out there. Do you have a job there?"

"Yes, I just got a coder position with Technophilia."

"I haven't heard about them," the Ambassador replied.

"Yeah, they're a smaller company," Erasmus noted, not entirely paying attention to what the Ambassador and Marie-Thérèse were saying. Out of the corner of his eye he could swear he could see Mrs. Inkpenne glide backward from the registration desk to the front office, without moving a muscle. *"Surely not..."* he thought.

A minute of thought later, Erasmus heard the dinner bell. One of the waiters came into the parlour form the front hall, "Ladies and Gentlemen, dinner is ready. Please follow me," he said, leading the crowd back into the dining room.

Mrs. Inkpenne stood within, alongside the kitchen door, silently staring at each of the guests. *"Something's not right about her this evening,"* Erasmus thought, noting how her skin seemed paler than normal, which frankly was a feat in itself. He began to think more in depth about what he knew about Mrs. Inkpenne, a. that her family had owned this inn since her ancestors built it before the Revolution, b. that she had to have been quite old, and c. that her best friend was her cousin Eleanor. "Marie-Thérèse," Erasmus said, putting a hand on her arm, "I think I know what's going on with Mrs. Inkpenne."

"What?"

"Look at her, just look."

Marie-Thérèse and Erasmus stopped and looked at the innkeeper, who gazed back at them, her tired gaze broken by a weak smile. « *Ce n'est pas vrai !* »[29] Marie-Thérèse gasped.

"It has to be, Honoria Inkpenne is a ghost!"

"Then her cousin Eleanor, could she be Eleanor Roosevelt?"

---

[29] "It's not true!"

"I think so," Erasmus said, pulling out his phone. He quickly found a picture of the same Eleanor and compared it to Mrs. Inkpenne, "They're definitely related. I can't believe it! She's a ghost."

"It all makes sense though. How else would we have seen the ghost of her as a young girl in the carriage house?" Marie-Thérèse asked.

"True, so true," Erasmus replied, turning his back on the phantom innkeeper, old Honoria Inkpenne, who had died in 1971, yet had never left her post as she had no children to pass the inn onto. Honoria watched on, happy with the knowledge that someone understood her. She was content.

Marie-Thérèse and Erasmus walked over to a table where their names could be found on place markers. Marie-Thérèse took a seat on the far side of the table, while Erasmus sat with his back to the kitchen. After a few moments, the waiters came out with the pre-prepared menus, each with three options, veal, lamb, or a vegan option. Erasmus and Marie-Thérèse chose the veal and found themselves enjoying immensely their dinner. All the wines that evening were imported from Australia, and were rich in flavour, just as much as the French and Austrian varieties that they had enjoyed the nights previously.

Yet Erasmus felt empty, somewhat vacant. The joy he ought to feel at dining with his love wasn't there. Instead there was a deep sadness, *"This time next week I'll be leaving her for California,"* he thought. One week. Seven days. The time that they had together was running by fast. Before he knew it, it would be over. He knew he would miss his evenings with Marie-Thérèse sitting in their living room on the Upper West Side, he knew he would miss her cooking, her jokes, and her company. He knew what he wanted to say, and that he should dare to say it.

He set down his fork and knife and looked up at her. Marie-Thérèse had been watching him, a similar apprehension in her eyes. There were things that she wanted to say, but was afraid to say them. All around them sat strangers, except perhaps for the Ambassador, people who they didn't know, and who after tomorrow would never see them again. But still there they sat, silently searching for words. Erasmus's brain was running faster than it had before, he couldn't wait any longer. He stood, silencing the room. Everyone around them had stopped eating, and were watching, wondering what was about to happen. Erasmus looked down at Marie-Thérèse, and put out his hand for her to take. She accepted it, and with a little help from her clumsy friend stood up and took his other hand in hers. They stood there, staring into each other's eyes, in the middle of the dining room.

Perhaps Erasmus spoke first, perhaps Marie-Thérèse, but whoever it was didn't matter then, and frankly doesn't matter now.

What does matter is what they said next. Erasmus looked deep into her eyes and said with all the clarity his voice could muster, *"Je t'aime,"* and she, at the same moment, "I love you." They kissed, deeply, fully, with the room around them bursting into applause.

Epilogue

Erasmus sat in the back of a taxi, moving at a decent speed through the Lincoln Tunnel. All his worldly possessions were in a pair of suitcases in the trunk, his life seemingly split into different places. Next to him sat Marie-Thérèse, her pale face glistening with the tears that she'd tried to hide from him. It was only going to be four months, the end of winter and all of spring, but four months still was too long to be apart. Erasmus didn't care to watch the sights of New York City go by as he left his home for the last six years. He didn't care that he was leaving the city often called the Capital of the World. For him, his world was in disarray. His life would be going west with him to California, but his love would stay here in the east.

"You'll videocall me as much as possible, right?" Erasmus asked.

"Of course, every day if you'd like."

Erasmus felt some relief.

"Do you have a place to live yet out there?" she asked.

"No, not yet. I'm going to stay with my Aunt Cecilia for a few weeks until I find a place."

"That'll be good, at least you'll have a roof over your head then."

"Yes, and it'll be dry in case it rains."

"Erasmus, it hasn't rained out there in a while."

"Really? I thought it rained every day in San Francisco."

Marie-Thérèse smiled at him, "Is that why you've been stocking up on umbrellas?"

"No, I was going to give my family umbrellas for Christmas."

"Why?"

"My grandfather always said, 'You can never go a day without a good umbrella.'"

Marie-Thérèse laughed, snorting loudly enough to catch the eye of the cabbie on the other side of the glass.

"What'd you get me for Christmas then?" she asked Erasmus.

"O, would you like to open it now, or save it for Christmas morning?"

She looked at a small box that he'd pulled out of his coat pocket. *"Wait, is he going to give me a ring? Right before he leaves? O no, I'm going to get a proposal in the back of a taxi in the Lincoln Tunnel ..."* she thought.

"How about now?"

"Sounds good to me," Erasmus replied, handing her the box. It was wrapped in a light grey paper with brown string holding everything together. "I got it at that jewellers that we like in Midtown."

Marie-Thérèse was silent, but her mind was racing away, *"He's really going to propose to me in the back of a taxi in the Lincoln Tunnel ..."*

"Well, are you going to open it?" he asked.

She unwrapped it, almost afraid of what would be inside. Beneath the grey paper was a box from Sforzano's, the jeweler in question. She looked at the lid for a moment, and let her gloved fingers pull it open. Inside wrapped in paper was something made of silver. She pulled back the paper and found all her fear evaporate at the sight of her Christmas present.

"Erasmus, I love you!" she said, kissing him deeply on the lips, holding her new silver umbrella lapel pin in hand. She pinned it onto the lapel of her coat and looked over to see Erasmus's face beaming with the biggest grin she'd seen yet. "What?" she asked, eyeing her look.

"You thought I was going to propose, didn't you."

She smiled, kissing him again, "Thank you for not proposing to me in the back of a taxi in the Lincoln Tunnel."

He laughed, "That would have been an idea. Your brother Charles mentioned tunnels as good places for a proposal."

"Wait, you talked to Charles?"

"O yeah, when you get to Newark, wait at the arrivals hall for a bit."

"Wait, you invited my family to come to New York for Christmas?"

"Of course, I figured you'd be a bit lonely out here alone in our, or rather your, apartment. Now there's an open bedroom."

"So who's coming?"

"Your parents, your brothers Charles and Pierre, and your sister Lucille."

"Where are they all going to sleep?" Marie-Thérèse asked.

"I figured your parents could take my bed –"

"And my siblings?"

"I borrowed some cots from that astrophysicist next door. She wants them back by the New Year."

Marie-Thérèse looked up at him, and nodded her head in an approving fashion, "Well done, Erasmus Plumwood. I think this'll be a nice Christmas after all."

He smiled, leaned over in the back seat and kissed her. "But it won't be a beautiful Christmas without you, M.T."

A tear dropped from her eyes. "I don't know what I'm going to do without you for these four months."

"You'll think of something, you're the smartest person I know. Have you started looking for jobs?"

"In San Francisco, yes. There's a *lycée* out there that is hiring a teacher. It sounds like something I could be good at."

"I think you could be good at anything you set your mind to."

She laughed, "And if you screw things up at Technophilia you can always become a motivational speaker."

"Yeah, tell them that they shouldn't worry about their self-worth, after all they don't trip on their own feet as much as me."

She laughed, leaning over onto his shoulder.

"You know your sister wants to go to the Met with you. She's never been," Erasmus said, leaning his head back onto hers, a hand on her shoulder.

"She'll love it; she's the artist in the family."

"And what about you? What do you want to do with them this Christmas?"

"I think I'll take them for a walk to the waterfall in Central Park, see what they think of it."

"That'll be nice," Erasmus replied.

"What'll you do with your parents?"

"O, I don't know. We'll probably go to Midnight Mass at Visitation, they always have a neat choir and a full orchestra."

Marie-Thérèse smiled, "Kansas City's a nice place to live. How'd you like to end up there?"

"Of all the places around the globe, Kansas City would be where I'd like to live."

"It's your home," she said.

"Home is where you are," he whispered into her ear.

The taxi was now in New Jersey, driving along the highway past billboard after billboard, hotel after hotel, ever closer to the airport. "Which terminal, sir?" the cabbie called back through the glass.

"Terminal 2 please," Erasmus replied.

They rounded their way into Newark's maze of roads and up to the drive in front of the departures hall at Terminal 2. "Here we are, that'll be $52," the cabbie said.

Erasmus reached for his wallet but felt a hand on his arm, "No, I'll pay for this. *Joyeux Noël,* »" Marie-Thérèse said, taking the bills from the wallet in her purse. She handed them to the driver through a small hole in the window, which earned his thanks, and then followed Erasmus out of the taxi. Collecting his luggage from the trunk, they walked into the departures hall. Down a flight of stairs from the check-in counters at the security checkpoint they stopped and turned to each other, "I'll see you in four months," Erasmus said, hugging Marie-Thérèse.

"That's too long," she replied, the tears falling even more on her cheeks.

"Just think, once the snows melt it'll be time to come west."

She leaned back and looked him in the eye, her voice bleary from her crying, "I love you, Erasmus Plumwood!"

« Je t'aime aussi, Marie-Thérèse Merlinais ! »[30]

As he walked into the security checkpoint, she stood there and watched until he was out of sight. Erasmus Plumwood had left New York, and their relationship, only just begun, would have to take a long-distance turn, if only for a while. Four months was a long time, but Napoléon had had just barely four months in power between Elba and Saint Helena. As Marie-Thérèse walked down to the arrivals hall below she knew she'd be seeing Erasmus Plumwood soon.

An alert buzzed in her phone in one of the chest pockets of her coat. She pulled it out from within and looked at the screen. It was a text from Erasmus, "Your family's on the 13:15 flight from Montréal."

Marie-Thérèse smiled, "Erasmus Plumwood, you're forgetful, your clumsy, your unobservant, but I do love you!"

---

[30] "I love you too, Marie-Thérèse Merlinais!"

ABOUT THE AUTHOR

The Author at Glen Ellis Falls, December 2017.

Seán Thomas Kane is a writer. He has written 14 plays to date, hundreds of poems and a good number of short stories. He is best known as a historian, political analyst, and as a polyglot. Kane lives in Kansas City, Missouri. This is his first novel.

www.ingramcontent.com/pod-product-compliance
Lightning Source LLC
Chambersburg PA
CBHW020752210626
46807CB00018B/3000